THIS SECRET DIARY BELONGS TO ALISTAIR FURY

Last day of the school term was a chamber of horrors. Miss Bird gave us homework for the holidays – may she find nothing but deadly piranha fish and men with poisonous blowpipes waiting for her on her British Waterways break on the Macclesfield Canal. She has given us a holiday diary to write. I mean, perlease! Who keeps a diary nowadays except giggly horsey-loving girls and saddoes with no friends!

But here it is – another hilarious instalment of *The War Diaries of Alistair Fury*, from award-winning writer, Jamie Rix.

www.**kidsatrandomhouse**.co.uk

Other titles in THE WAR DIARIES OF
ALISTAIR FURY series, published by Corgi
Yearling Books:

Bugs on the Brain

Dead Dad Dog

The Kiss of Death

Tough Turkey

Also by Jamie Rix, in Young Corgi Books:

One Hot Penguin

Mr Mumble's Fabulous Flybrows

THE WAR DIARIES OF ALISTAIR FURY

SUMMER HELLIDAY

JAMIE RIX

Illustrated by Nigel Baines

CORGI YEARLING BOOKS

THE WAR DIARIES OF ALISTAIR FURY: *SUMMER HELLIDAY*
A CORGI YEARLING BOOK : 0 440 86591 3

Published in Great Britain by Corgi Books,
an imprint of Random House Children's Books

This edition published 2004

3 5 7 9 10 8 6 4 2

Set in 12/14.5pt Comic Sans by
Falcon Oast Graphic Art Ltd.

Corgi Books are published by Random House Children's Books,
61–63 Uxbridge Road, London W5 5SA,
a division of The Random House Group Ltd,
in Australia by Random House Australia (Pty) Ltd,
20 Alfred Street, Milsons Point, Sydney, NSW 2061,
Australia,
in New Zealand by Random House New Zealand Ltd,
18 Poland Road, Glenfield, Auckland 10, New Zealand
and in South Africa by Random House (Pty) Ltd,
Endulini, 5a Jubilee Road, Parktown 2193, South Africa

THE RANDOM HOUSE GROUP LIMITED REG. NO. 954009
www.kidsatrandomhouse.co.uk

Printed and bound in Great Britain by
Cox & Wyman Ltd, Reading, Berkshire.

For Milo,
who makes Alistair look positively angelic

EVERY DAYS IN EVERY WAYS I'M SAVING THE PLANET FROM HARMFUL RAYS!

This ECO-diary belongs to – Alistair Fury

Age – 11.

Address – 47 Atrocity Road, Tooting, England

Favourite Flower – Poisoned Ivy or Hemlock

• **Favourite Tree** – Willow, because it makes great bats to bash evil big brothers and sisters with.

Favourite Animal – Not Mr E our pukey pug dog & not Napoleon our unbalanced cat. My favourite animal is a KILLER BEE! I know it sounds little and silly, but it is more worse than a shark for killing people. This is because there are more killer bees nearer to humans than there are sharks. I mean how many picnics have you been on when a swarm of white sharks has descended on your fairy cakes? Good point, Alistair. Perhaps with your amazing powers of deduction (and handsome nose) you should join

7

the police going straight in at rank of
Sherlock Holmes!

BEES ARE COOL AND
SO ARE BEETLES
POWER TO THE LITTLE
PEOPLES!!!

Favourite Eco-Charities – Freds of the
Earth (what I don't understand is how a
Society of Freds can have a man called
Jonathan[1] in charge), Greenpeas, I'm Nasty
International, the National Rust, CND
(Campaign for Non Distressing of me).

**Person You Most Admire After Alan
Titchmarsh** – Apart from his daughter
Charlie Dimmock, who is an obvious choice,
I would have to say – Don Bellini, inven-
tor of the Concrete Overcoat, which for a
period in 1920s was more popular than the
Macintosh. But the Concrete Overcoat was
too heavy and people kept falling off
bridges into rivers and sinking, so it was
taken out of shops, leaving a gap in the

---

[1] Jonathan Porridge for those of you ignorants in the
No-Know!

market for Donkey Jackets. But donkeys hated wearing jackets so the coat factories switched to making Anoraks instead - which are made from the nylon fleece of the Tibetan Rak, I believe.

List Your Plans to Save Our Planet – Put a plug up my big brother whose farts not only blow holes in his jeans but blow holes in the ozone layer too.

We hold our planet in trust for future generations. What are the guiding principles that help you to live your life in harmony with nature? – If it moves shoot it. If it looks at you in a suspect way, shoot it. If it blows in the wind, or smells funny or dares to block your lovely view of nature's glorious bounty, shoot it and bury it out of sight.

Notes

'O glorious summer' - many great poets have written about the summer. William Shakespeare himselfeth wrote: 'Now is the summer of our disco tent, where the Duke of York had his 40th birthday bash.' And was it not Wordsworth who wrote famously about a sea of daffodils pushing up towards the sun through sloshy cowpats?

Yes, summer is the best time of the year, because I can get out of the house and escape the murderous clutches of my big brother and sister who shun the sun like vampires. My big brother doesn't like the sun in case it dries up his spots and makes him look attractive. And my big sister is such a fat blob she refuses to wear a bikini, because she says her stomach hangs down to her knees. She's not wrong - she looks like a human boa-constrictor who's just eaten a baby hippo. Also this summer we are going on a brilliant holiday to Spain, which is a phat place for revenges apparently. There are bulls everywhere. So I have secretly bought a red rag, which I shall cunningly pin to the back of my big brother and sister's T-shirts when we see our first angry bull on the streets of Torremolinos! kersplat! Ulay!

Last day of term tomorrow – quarter day really. Only in school for two hate-filled hours to say untruths like 'happy holidays' and 'really hope you don't drown in a freak white-water rafting accident over the Niagara Falls' to a bunch of teachers who hate children and are hated back with knobs on. So *today* is the last day really. Why school doesn't let us off one day early and save our weary brains tomorrow I will never know! Actually then today

Believe me, I'm very weary

Brain goo

would be the last day so they'd have to let us off yesterday. Then yesterday would be the last day so they'd have to let us off the day before yesterday ... What a spunky-monkey idea! Eventually we wouldn't have to go to school at all! Life would be one long lazy summer holiday. Howzat! Strawberries and cream! Hayfever!

Miss Bird has said we can bring games in today. Have brought Mum's laptop and my

That's Aaron, Ralph and me - we are the grit that gets in your swimming trunks on the beach and gives you a rash on your unmentionables!

new webcam. Webcam cost me load of wonga-wonga that I was saving to muck up big sister Mel's love life. She is a Txt maniac. Without phone she would have no boyfriends. My brilliant plan was to cut out her mobile phone signal by secretly lining her bedroom with roofing lead. Tried test bit over bed, but Blu-tak failed. Lead fell off in middle of afternoon and put Boyfriend Number 1032 in hospital with high voice and no chance of children, which was probably for best as he was butt-ugly anyway. Besides, webcam offers opportunity for spying, which is much more immoral!

Revengers slid cam under loo doors and saw three people sitting on the loo! Actually excitement wears off after first time, because all you can see are shoes and wrinkled pants. Aaron and Ralph wanted to

push it under door when Miss Bird was in there, but who wants to see hairy legs with fleas on? I can see that at home with big brother, Will. Ralph put cam up nostril so we could see his bogeys and Aaron put it in his mouth so we could see his voice talking.

It got stuck. Nurse had to slide it out by lining Aaron's mouth with soap. Saw what Aaron had had for breakfast after that.

At home, Mum busy making phone calls. She has three weeks to come up with new cookery programme or the BBC will give her a free transfer to ITV to host a new celebrity quiz show called *I'm a Celebrity Cook Get Me Out of this Cannibal's Cook Pot*. For some reason she's not keen.

Dad was out and Granny was playing Scrabble with herself in the sitting room.

She is sad. Words so far: MISERY, WEEP, EMPTY and JANXY.

'What's Janxy?' I asked.

'Sixty points,' she said. 'It's on a triple letter word.'

'You can't just make up words, Granny,' I said. 'The whole point is to do words that exist.'

'Of course Janxy exists,' she blushed. 'It's ... It's the nectar feather of a hummingbird. It's a tiny tail feather that looks like a scary face and frightens off other hummingbirds while the greedy hummingbird's got his real face stuffed up to his ears in a flower.' Hummingbirds don't have ears otherwise all that humming would drive them bonkers. She is the

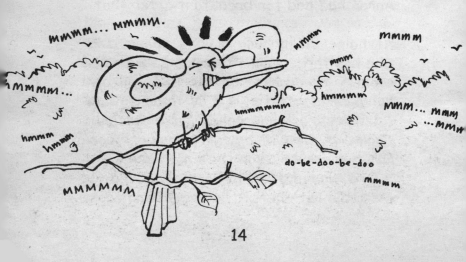

MMMM... MMMM.
MMMM
nmm
mmm
MMMM...
hmmmm
MMM... mmm
...MMM
hmmm
hmmm
mmmmmmm
do-be-doo-be-doo
MMMMMM
mmmm

14

Oh the memory of it makes me feel sick

biggest lying cheat in the world and hides court cards in her underwear.

To pay her back for her sins we told her we could read minds and proved it by sitting in front of her and telling her what letters she had in her hand.

'MUHLOBE,' I said. She could have made BUMHOLE but that's rude and Scrabble is a game for decent church-going folk so I didn't help her. Granny was impressed and called me Madame Alistair, which I did not find funny. 'I am not a girl!' I said. I am not a mind reader either. We just hid the cam on the mantelpiece behind her and read the letters over her shoulder. She did wonder why I needed a computer on my lap and a wire leading out the back of the computer, across the carpet and into a bunch of dried flowers in a vase on the mantelpiece, but I think she believed my excuse:

'This computer is powered by dried flowers instead of batteries, Granny. And I need the computer, because I am the American President's right-hand man. This computer fires the nuclear bomb. I have to be attached to it at all times in case he calls and wants it dropping.'

Mr President

Pushed cam under big brother's bedroom door, but couldn't see much due to fug and gloom. Heard him shuffling and grunting like a troll. Will has become a Neanderthal caveman. All he needs is a loincloth and a pair of strap-on bootees made from the kidneys of a dinosaur and he could fit into a Stone Age family. We pushed J-cloth and flip-flops under door, which was nearest we could find. It is since he stopped washing that Will has been smelling like a primitive man. He won't touch water. He just stares at himself in the bathroom mirror and squeezes spots. Also, he doesn't speak any more. I think that when his voice broke it must have broken for ever. He should have got it mended.

Mel was in her bedroom snogging, or should I say eating, Boyfriend Number 1033, Tarquin – apparently he's going to be a famous actor one day when he's got some talent. I think he's already the best actor in the world, because my big sister actually believes that he likes her!

NO 1033

17

Unfortunately we got too bold with spy-cam. We pushed it nearer bed to get closer look at saucy lip action. Ralph wanted to pick up some hot tips. Mel saw something move across the floor, thought it was a rat, screamed and leaped off the bed with Tarquin's tongue still in her mouth. He had to rush home for an ice pack and tongue plaster while Mel had

screaming habjabs. She called me and my friends 'dirty little peeping toms with the minds of dead hedgehogs and the manners of bears doing you-know-what in the woods!' I told her I'd remember that.

'To pay me back later?' she sneered.

'No,' I said. 'It makes us sound well hard.'

That is the greatest job in the world. You are paid to peep through walls at girls!

Then she put her hands on her hips and said,'Right! I've got a huge secret that I *was* going to tell you, Alice, but now I'm *not*.'

Spoilsport! I *love* secrets. Knowing someone's secrets, whether they know you know or not, is like being a cameraman on *Big Brother*!

So not knowing a secret, that I now knew was being kept secret from me, gnawed away at my mental stability.

A MEDICAL THOUGHT AND GENEROUS CONTRIBUTION TO THE FUTURE OF MANKIND ABOUT MENTAL STABILITY

If madness runs in the family, change your family. End of madness. End of family. Double result. Alistair wins Nobel Prize and quite right too.

The Son

Rooting in Tooting for our noble Alistair

Not dangle-monster. The flannel. If he'd chucked my dangle-monster out of the window I wouldn't be writing this now. I would be bandaged in hospital with an invitation from the Girl Guides to join up!

Had hot bath to calm down. Was blowing up duck with underwater nuclear fart bubbles when door burst open. Will pinned me down while Mel filmed me with Dad's video camera. Tried to cover dangle-monster with flannel, but Will chucked it out of the window.

When I got out of bath, heard hoots of laughter from Mel's bedroom. Banged on locked door but big brother and sister wouldn't let me in.

'Frut garn,' grunted Will. Took ten minutes to work out what he'd said – front garden.

To say I was humiliated would be exactly right. To pay me back for spying they had rigged up a TV screen in Mel's bedroom window overlooking the street, and were playing the video of me naked in the bath to passersby! Over the window they had strung a sheet on which they had painted the message:

HOOT iF YOU THiNK HE'S GOT A BiG WiLLY

In the two minutes I was standing on the path, I counted twenty-three cars go past. None of them hooted.

Then, just as I was turning to run indoors, one did! I was so happy I cried.

'Thank you,' I shouted, turning to wave at the car ... only, there wasn't a car. Just an old lady walking a tortoise. The road was empty. The honker was Mel hanging out the window with a car horn in her hand.

'You really are a *little* brother!' she shouted. **'HONK! HONK!'**

Have gone to bed bitter and twisted. My big brother and sister have wrecked my whole summer holiday ALREADY! For this act

of unspeakable cruelty I now declare a summer war. I shall show no mercy. I shall fight them on the beaches and water down their suncream till they burn!

FRIDAY (DAY 0)

Chamber of horrors of chamber of horrors! Last day at school was a chamber of horrors. *Horrors* because Miss Bird gave us homework for the holiday – may she find nothing but deadly piranha fish and men with poisonous blowpipes waiting for her on her British Waterways break on the Macclesfield Canal – and *chamber of* because, like a chamberpot, she stinks. She has given us a holiday diary to write. I mean, perlease! Who keeps a diary nowadays? Nobody except giggly horsey-loving girls and saddoes with no friends!

After Miss Bird had left the classroom, us Revengers made our protest loud and clear via Operation Compost! We filled her

desk full of rotting stuff so it will smell like a cow's nappy when she comes back in September! Wet leaves, pond weed, six pots of yoghurt, blue cheese, an ugly fish from the school kitchen, football socks and Aaron's special brew of bottled egg and lumpy milk mix! Then we ran out of school and didn't look back till we reached home.

On the way, we discussed stuff. We were going to be apart for three weeks. How would we communicate if revenges needed cooking up? Postcards could be read by the enemy and were too slow to arrive; messages in bottles arrived a bit faster than postcards, but were prone to oil-tanker collisions in the Persian Gulf; and pigeon post was unreliable over France.

'Why?' said Aaron.

'Because they eat everything in France,' I said. 'The pigeon would be shot down over Paris and in a pot faster than you could say, "Waiter, there's a postcard in my soup!"'

'I've got it!' gasped Ralph. 'Webcam! I'll buy the kit!'

LIFE LESSON WHICH WE'D ALL DO WELL TO LEARN FROM

This is a **FACT!** Ralph may be thick and less intelligent than his school desk, but he's loaded. He's going to Barbados for his holiday, while Aaron's staying here and I'm only going to Spain. Which proves that even thick people get money and when they've got it they generally go on better holidays. It still makes me sick, but there it is.

In meantime needed horrible revenge for big brother and sister. We decided to bide our time like Japanese Hunting Turtles and find out Mel's secret by using

Cammo – my new nickname for webcam. Have called it Cammo because it's a bit like *ammo* (deadly) with a C on the front for 'All C-ing Eye!' (and camera, obviously). Quite clever really. The plan was staggering in its sophistication.

Stage 1: Discover her secret.
Stage 2: Wreck it.

Walked into kitchen to find Mum happy. She was dancing and waving a glass of wine in the air. She pinched my cheeks and told me she loved me.

'That hurts,' I said.

'Well, love does hurt, Alistair!' She laughed in a rather wild and unsettling way.

Aaron and Ralph fell back against the kitchen units and clung onto the handles for safety. I asked why she was so happy, but she wouldn't say. It's another secret. **AAAAAAGGGGGGHHHHHH!!!!!!!!!!**

What is it with this family and secrets? Why won't anyone talk to me? Am starting to feel like Mr E, our pukey pug dog, who is *never* told the truth. 'Shall we go for a lovely walk?' means let's go see the nurse for a painful injection! 'What's that food on the floor?' means bend over while I insert this worm powder up your bottom! And the worst of the lot – 'Is that a naughty pussy cat I can see on the ceiling, Mr E?' means hold still while the vet cuts off your testicles!

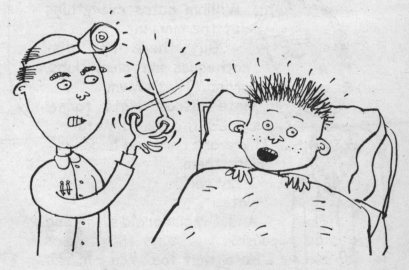

ALISTAIR'S EMERGENCY TESTICLE CHECK JUST IN CASE MUM'S SECRET WAS THAT SHE HAD TAKEN ME TO THE VET WITHOUT ME KNOWING AND GIVEN ME THE *NUTS-AWAY* OPERATION TO CALM ME DOWN
No worries. Both there.

Unfortunately, Mel was out buying more summer clothes for Spain. Mum and Dad are going to have to hire an extra jumbo jet just to carry her suitcases. William on the other hand has no clothes for Spain. Why?

'Hate Spain. Not going.' William hates everything at the moment.

'But there are discotheques and foamy clubs, darling.' That's Mum.

'Hate discos. Hate foamy clubs.' He's into Death Metal.

'There are bars and beaches.'

'Hate them.'

'Crazy golf.'

'Hate it.'

'And McDdonald's.' Long pause.

'Hate that too.' You can tell he doesn't really.

Waited till Mel got back from shops and disappeared into bedroom for lunch with Tarquin – tongue sandwich, of course – before sliding Cammo under door.

28

To our surprise, enemy had launched counter-measures. There were socks stuffed in the crack. Did they think we were amateurs? Did they think we hadn't planned a counter-measure to counter their counter-measure? We got the tooth mug from the bathroom and listened through the wall. These were the words I heard Mel speak. The ones I couldn't hear very clearly are in brackets.

'Oooh! GIGGLE! Can you (rally)? A film audition? Tomorrow (moaning)? I don't believe it. SQUEAL OF DELIGHT! (meat) an actress! You're a (mason)! And I'm going to be (a mouse)! Oh Tarquin, I (lump) you. I (lump) you. I (lump) you more than (hairy)-thing in the world. It's my (cream) come (too).'

So that was her huge secret! Tarquin had got Mel an audition for a film.

'Do you think it's selling ice creams in the interval?' asked Aaron.

'No,' I said, 'it's acting.'

'Is she any good?'

'If you put her in a Tweenies costume

and got someone else to say her lines she'd still be worse than awful,' I said.

Ralph had a cracking idea on how to stitch her up.

PLAN A – STUFF UP MEL

'We go to the audition and make her laugh in the middle of her speech,' he said. 'They never give prizes to gigglers.'

'But she's a misery-guts,' I said. 'She never laughs.'

'Everyone laughs at something,' said Ralph. 'What's funny?'

'Farts,' said Aaron. 'They kill me.'

'Me too,' I said. 'Farts.'

'OK, farts,' said Ralph. 'What else?'

We sat in silence for forty-five minutes but couldn't think of another thing.

It didn't matter. Mum put her boot into our brilliant idea.

PPPHHHT

TTTHRUMP

Just once I'd like to be taken seriously!!

'You can't go!' she said.

'But Mel—'

'Is older than you.'

'But it's an open audition,' I told her. 'Anyone can go.'

'Not you,' she said. 'I disapprove of child actors. Money turns them peculiar. They start wanting houses of their own and flashy cars and divorces from their parents.' Sounded good to me.

NO FREE
PAPERS
OF
PARENTS

PLAN B – DIVORCE WHOLE FAMILY

I have changed my mind. Instead of going to mess up Mel, I'm going to get myself a

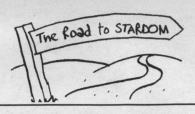

part! Without wishing to be modest, I have always suspected that I was born to be a celebrity. Something about my lovely hair and dazzling good looks, not to mention my love of money and cheap publicity. I had to get Mum to change her mind.

'Please,' I said. 'I won't pee in the bidet again if you let me audition.' She looked stunned. I suspect that was the first she'd ever heard of my bidet activities. And *she* used the bidet every day as part of her deep-pore facial cleansing routine.

Just then, Dad rushed through the kitchen, lock-ing the door behind him and shutting all the cur-tains and blinds until we were standing in the dark.

'What are you doing?' said Mum, switch-ing the light on.

Dad's face was grey. He was sweaty scared.

'Are you being hunted by the police?' I asked.

Dad grabbed me by the shoulders and shook me so hard that I thought my jaw might fall off. 'Tell me what you know!' he screamed.

'You're h ... h ... h ... h ... h ... urt ... t ... t ... ting my t ... t ... t ... t ... eeth,' I said.

Suddenly the doorbell rang. He dropped me on the floor, ran into the hall, grabbed an umbrella off the table, leaned his back against the front door and cocked his head  over his shoulder to speak – a bit like James Bond, only *not* like James Bond, because Dad's got a body like Fido Dido.

'What do you want?' he said.

'Pizza,' said the voice outside.

'Prove it!' said Dad. There was a pause.

What is a jury?

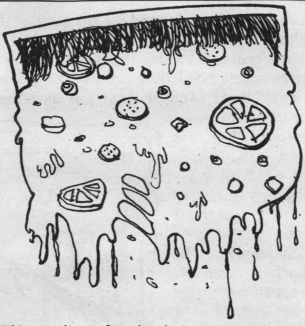

Then a slice of melted pizza was squeezed through the letter box. Dad pulled open the door, grabbed the box, put a fiver into the motorcyclist's hand and slammed the door again. The pizza was William's. Now he'd stopped *eating* with his family as well.

'What do you think you're doing?' Mum asked Dad, as he put on sunglasses.

'I've bunked off Jury Service,' he said.

'But I thought you only agreed to do it because you got time off work.'

'I did,' he said. 'But when I got to court,

34

the judge said the case was going to take at least *six* weeks and we had to be in *every* day from nine till five. That's like harder work then work! So I told them I was ill and got off. But when I was leaving the court this policeman gave me a dirty look like I was a toe-rag who was going to get what was coming to me. It's only a matter of time before the police find me and drag me off to prison. I'm in trouble, girl. Big trouble.'

Not as much as I was. Mum had cooked Wild Hedgehog Cutlets for supper and I was the only one who hadn't eaten – William had his pizza, Mel had Tarquin, Dad had lost his appetite to fear, the Revengers had their own suppers to get back to, and Mum never ate anything she'd cooked in case she didn't like it.

Couldn't face a whole hedgehog on my own so asked Granny round for supper. She'll eat anything after living through the war and rationing. I knew it meant more Scrabble but it was a sacrifice worth making. After all, a hedgehog shared is a hedgehog halved.

erm...
WHAT??!!

Mum started to love me again when I ate her hedgehog, so I asked politely if she'd changed her mind.

'Are you sure I can't audition to-morrow?' I said. She still said no. So I went for sympathy. I pretended to have a heart attack and as my dying wish I whispered that I wanted to audition for the film. Mum ignored me. I lay there for hours, slumped across the table with my face in the Cordon Bleu Roadkill. Eventually, I sat back up.

'You should thank your mother,' said Granny. 'She's just saved you from making a big professional mistake, Alistair. Don't take this the wrong way, but your heart attack was rubbish. I've seen better acting on a football pitch. A real heart attack looks like this.' Then she rolled her eyes up to the top of her head, clutched her left shoulder and fell forward into her hedgehog.

Mum sighed and left the table. So I did the same.

12 p.m. Midnight – Everyone in bed. Was just woken by Granny ordering a cab in the hall. Then she slammed down the telephone, opened the front door and shouted, 'That *could* have been a *real* heart attack. You didn't know. You're just waiting for me to die to get your grubby hands on my money, aren't you? I'm only good for one thing – looking after your pets while you go gallivanting around the world on holiday. Well . . . I'm at the end of my life, aren't I? I've nearly got *two* feet in the grave! What could I possibly want with a two-week holiday of a lifetime in Spain? Goodnight!'

Granny's memory must have stopped working. She's already had four holidays this year. Five, if you count belly dancing in Morocco.

What is a Jury?

I phoned Ralph later and asked his dad, the Rev. Ming. He says that a jury is twelve people who sit in a court of law, listen to both sides of a case and decide whether the accused is innocent or guilty. Weird! If the bloke's accused he must have done it. That sort of injustice would never work in the Revengers. It's much quicker to decide someone's guilty then go out and do him.

SATURDAY
(DAY 1 OF HOLIDAYS)

Dreamed I was a celebrity last night.

MY SUNBEAM DREAM OF ME IN THE LAND OF CELEBRITY

I was living in my glittering ring-fenced country mansion. My life was complete except for lack of personal hairdresser. I was throwing a masked ball for six hundred other celebrities in the hope that one of them would give me their hairdresser as a present. I laid on dancing sea lions, ice sculptures of footballers' tattoos, teeth-whitening stalls, platypus beaks

in aspic, fire-breathing midgets. You name it, if it was in bad taste it was there. At the end of party, the guests had gone and I was swimming in champagne, when a solitary figure stepped out of the shadows and approached the pool, like B. Pitt in Meet Joe Black.

'Mr Alistair?' he said.

'Yes?' I said cautiously. Celebrities are naturally nervous of ordinary people, who are often mad and want to stab them with pens.

'I see blue highlights,' he said. And all at once I knew that my life was going to be perfect.

My Life

Sadly dreams are not like the real world. My life was pants and everyone else's was brilliant. Mel was swanking around the kitchen like a movie star. Nobody was allowed to use the phone in case Steven Spielberg called to wish her luck. And she was texting Tarquin on her mobile with messages like: WHEREMYFLWERS? and WHERERMYGOODLUCKCARDS? and WHEREISMY-CHAMPAIN? I didn't realize that Tarquin was one of the stars of this film. Maybe I'll have to be nice to him after all. Although obviously I would prefer to feed my own liver to a tapeworm!

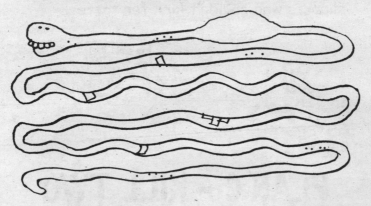

Will just spoke! It was a moment as historic as Jesus healing that leper with Savlon. Will told me that he hated acting, but hated me even more, which was why he was going to audition too. Mel has put him up to this! This is a despicable conspiracy to make me feel little.

'But you don't speak any more,' I said. 'How can you be an actor if you don't speak?'

'I can be a silent actor,' said William. 'Anyway, I *can* speak, when I want to.'

So I took a run up and kicked him in the bum and said, 'What do you say to that, then?'

And he said, 'Ooh ow!' like it hadn't hurt him at all. Like I was just a small ant in slippers who couldn't kick for toffee!

PLAN C – KILL TWO BIRDS WITH TWO FART CUSHIONS

Phoned Revengers in funk. Told them to meet me at lunch time outside Territorial Army Hall where auditions were taking place. Told them to bring double the amount of fart cushions as we now had *two*

scumbags to make laugh during their speeches.

Very cross when went off to piano lesson with the festering Mrs Muttley. To pay my whole family back I shall touch her skin and catch one of her seeping diseases. If I died of wartiness they'd all be sorry! Or maybe I could catch a verruca on my head. Instead of its little black roots burrowing into my foot, they would burrow into my brain and make me mad. Then I could do unmentionable things to my horrible family and they couldn't send me to prison. I'd be known as the Verruca Revenger.

I didn't know warthogs could have feelings for human beings!

Good plan.

Mrs Muttley was scary. She had brushed her teeth and washed her feet for the first time *ever*. Her dress was bright purple with spotted red pockets and a white frilly collar like a clown's. Her hair was dyed pink. She kept standing up, jumping towards the ceiling like a ballet dancer and singing an ear-piercing opera note that made my eyeballs wobble. I couldn't work out what was wrong with her.

'Are you *happy*?' I asked.

It was worse than that. She was *in love*!

Turned out she was playing the piano for the auditions for Mel's film and had fallen in love with the director!

Not only that but she was playing this lunch time! Not only that but she could get me in to see the director! Not only that but I'd only have to do a little something

44

With a long barge pole obviously.

for her in return! I told her I'd do anything so long as tongues weren't involved
or marzipan, because I hate marzipan.

What she wanted was rather old-
fashioned and sweet. If she got me an
audition and set me on the road to fame,
fortune and celebrityhood, I would put in
a good word for her with the director. If
she scratched my back, I'd scratch hers.

PLAN D –
GET RICH AND
FAMOUS AND DON'T
GIVE FAMILY A BEAN

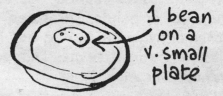

1 bean
on a
v. small
plate

Have decided to revenge myself against my
whole family at once by becoming a celebrity
and not inviting them to my parties.

Actually it sounded like she was blindfolded when she played it!

First Mrs Muttley had to teach me to sing. The film was an all-singing, all-dancing extravaganza. This came as something of a shock. I had seen myself as a good-looking actor in close-up all the time, not a gurning clown with happy-springs in my shoes. Never mind. We had to choose a song. I was all for doing that rap masterpiece *Slap My Bitch Up* but she didn't know the notes, so we settled on *Stand By Your Man* by Dolly Parton, which she could play blindfolded.

Read first lines, got worried: '*Sometimes it's hard to be a woman, giving all your love to just one man.*'

'Isn't that what a girl would sing?' I said, imagining the ribbing Ralph and Aaron would give me.

'The road to celebrity is a hard and rocky one,' she replied, 'strewn with abandoned principles. Besides it's the director's favourite and he has to notice *you* before he'll notice *me*.' That settled it. *Stand By Your Man* it was.

HOW TO BECOME A CELEBRITY — LESSON ONE

Abandon your principles. Do *anything* to get to the top. Kill your own grandmother if you have to. Write rude words on her Scrabble board and shock her to death!

HOW TO BECOME A CELEBRITY — LESSON TWO

While you are abandoning your principles, never stop smiling. If you think of celebrity as a car, smiling is like the petrol and wheels all rolled into one. It keeps the car on the road to the Celebrity Motel in the heart of Celebrityville.

HOW TO BECOME A CELEBRITY — LESSON THREE

On the road to Celebrityville, don't stop to pick up hitchhikers. They will slow you down and eat your travel sweets.

Back at home, Dad had dressed up in Mum's old clothes to throw police dogs off his scent. He let me in then locked the door behind me. I told Mum what I was doing and said she couldn't stop me. She said I could audition as many times as I liked, but if I was offered a part she wouldn't let me take it. Told Will I thought Mum was pathetic. He stopped talking to the mirror and squeezed a spot instead.

'No, she isn't,' he said. Pop!

'You're all pathetic,' I said.

'No, we're not,' he said. Pop!

'Yes, you are,' I said. 'I can't wait to go to Spain, because then I won't be cooped up with you losers all day.'

'Yes, you will,' he said. Pop!

So I said, 'Get a life, Will. When did you turn into Mr Boring-Brown-Slacks? All you ever do these days is say the opposite to what anyone else says.'

'No, I don't,' he said.

Last thing I wanted as a dancer was tired legs, so begged Dad for lift to audition. He couldn't leave the house without plastic surgery apparently, in case he was recognized by the police. Offered to trim his ears with pinking shears and reshape his nose with the iron, but he wouldn't play ball.

zZZZZZZz

Aaaagh! Someone find me a doctor to put me back! I wish I had never been born!

To make matters worse Mum said, 'If you're going to walk, Alistair, you can take Mr E with you.'

'But you're not doing anything,' I protested.

'Oh yes I am,' she winked. 'I'm doing something secret!'

Mr E was well behaved during walk to audition. Nothing squirted out of him when it shouldn't. He queued politely for an hour with all the other kids, including the delightful Pamela Whitby. If I'd been kinder I'd have told them all to go home. After all, none of them stood a chance with me singing the director's favourite song. But when Tarquin ushered Mel, Will and me into the audition room with twenty other children, Mr E lost his grip. It must have been the excitement of so many smelly ballet shoes. He slipped his lead, cocked his leg on Mrs Muttley's piano and made a middle sea on the floorboards. Then he trotted into the centre of the dance floor, where a heavy girl in an industrial boiler suit was performing the dance of the Dying Swan, and was sick under her feet. As she descended from a *pas de chat*, she slipped in the puddle of

It might have been a dying emu actually. Whatever it was, it was a hell of a big bird!

50

chunks, crashed to the ground and burst into tears. The director glared at me like I was scum and I saw my one chance of celebrityhood disappearing down the common drain.

I took Mr E outside into the car park, rang Aaron and Ralph and told them that I had an emergency and if they wanted to share in my upcoming wealth they had to get down here now to look after the dog.

'And why aren't you here anyway?' I said. 'It's nearly lunch time.' Aaron couldn't find

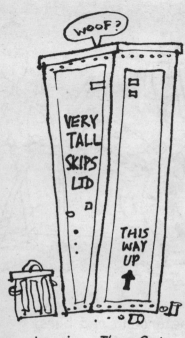

WOOF?

VERY TALL SKIPS LTD

THIS WAY UP ↑

his fart cushion. 'Forget the fart cushion,' I said. 'Just get down here now for dog-sitting!'

Thirty seconds later, they still hadn't turned up. So I dumped Mr E in a high-sided skip, yelled, 'Stay, boy! Stay!' and prayed that today wasn't pick-up day for high-sided skips!

Got back just as Mel was standing up to sing *I've Got a Brand New Combine Harvester* by the Wurzels. I sat down right in front of her so she couldn't help but see me and pretended that she'd got a big bogey hanging out the end of her nose. That messed up the first verse while she covered her face with her hand and mumbled the words. Then I did the funny 'Ugh! What is that disgusting smell!' face and pointed at her. She'd just started dancing and thought that with all the effort she'd squeaked one out by mistake, which made her forget her words. But I saved my best till last. Just as she was going for the big finish – '*I've got twenty acres* . . .' and all that stuff – I looked horrified. I gasped at her tights. 'Tear!' I mouthed, pointing at her bum. 'Tights are torn!' She thought her bum was hanging out at the back, stopped the song before she'd reached the end, covered herself up and rushed back to the climbing bars to sit down.

William was a doddle. He mucked *himself* up. When they asked who he was, he made such a mess of 'Hello, my name is William,' that the director didn't even ask him to sing.

'Hoe my nasal *what*?' he said. 'Forget it. Sit down!'

Just before my name was called, Tarquin came in with tea for the director.

As he crossed the hall he smiled at Mel, who was doing that look-at-poor-miserable-me crying that is so pathetic. Then the director spat his tea across the room and shouted, 'Where's my sugar, moron?' before kicking Tarquin in his walk-on part and sending him out to make some more. Not 100 per cent sure any more that Tarquin is the star he's said he is.

My turn. Leaped up and smiled at Mrs Muttley, who had been smiling all through the session in fact. Especially at the director, who never smiled back. She had changed her clothes to impress him and was now wearing yellow leggings with an emerald-green T-Shirt that said I'M HUGGABLE! Debatable – you'd need arms the length of a pre-stretched gorilla to reach round her waist.

Anyway, director took a couple of minutes to explain that the film was a bit like

54

Billy Elliot in as much as it followed the extraordinary story of Toopac Nijinski, a Tooting-born lad who, against all the odds, became a ballet dancer.

'So what are you going to give us, Alistair?'

'*Stand By Your Man*,' I said.

The director raised an eyebrow. 'Maybe I should call you Alice!' he joked.

I thought, Just you try it, mate, and I'll revenge myself on you till you're dancing with worms! What I actually said was, 'Yeah, right. Very funny.' Sometimes I embarrass myself.

I was rubbish at the song, because all the other boys were tittering, and I fell over twice during the dance routine when my legs accidentally moved in opposite directions. I ended with a breakdance spin and got a splinter in my neck. The director said thank you and I sat back down.

After everyone had done their bit, and Mrs Muttley had smeared bright red lipstick across her cheek from trying to eat a secret pasty between acts, the director said, 'Everyone can go except Pamela Whitby and Alistair Fury.'

You could have knocked me down with a feather. Several of the losing children didn't have a feather so they used their fists instead, before rushing out of the room in tears. That included Mel and Will!

It didn't bother me, because you know what Richard and Judy say:

'A loser will never a celebrity be. But a winner to Celebrityville is given the key.'

Sweet!

The gorgeous Pamela Whitby didn't seem that happy to have got the part though. I was playing Toopac and she was playing Trish, my childhood sweetheart.

'Bleurgh!' she said. 'I'm not kissing Alistair Fury even if it is essential to the plot!'

'Not even if I pay you a million pounds?' smiled the director.

'Not even if you make him wear a Prince William mask!' she said.

I didn't want to look hurt so I said,'I wouldn't want to kiss you anyway, fart-face, because I hate girls!'

And when the director said, 'Good,' I wondered what he meant.

I wanted to know if we were really

This is a lie, but nobody must tell her.

57

getting a million pounds each. He smiled again and said he didn't know how much we were getting paid, which I thought was a bit cheesy.

'You *are* both free to make this film, aren't you?' he asked.

Pamela was, but I was going to Spain in two weeks.

'Erm ... when were you thinking of shooting?' I asked casually.

'Next weekend,' he said.

'For how long?'

'As long as it takes,' he said. 'Two, three days!' It was a miracle! I could do it!

After we'd shaken on the deal, I tried

to have a man-to-man word with the director about his feelings for Mrs Muttley. I tried to talk her up, but it was hard finding nice things to say.

'She's been very clean recently and knows several tunes on the piano,' I said. 'And when she opens her mouth to sing it's very funny because her throat looks like the entrance to a big black coal pit with a little pink miner waving in the middle.' I paused to scratch my brain for more gems. 'She's got lovely floral dress sense. Bees like her. And she puts a lot of lipstick on. Anyway, she loves you and wants to know if you love her back.'

The director just laughed. The laugh started off funny, then turned spooky, then psychotic. I left.

William called me a girl when I walked into the car park. I told him he was just jealous that I could act and he couldn't even say his own name.

'Not correct actually, Alice,' he said. 'It is a well-known fact that all actors want to be girls – otherwise why would they wear make-up in front of the cameras?'

'Russell Crowe doesn't want to be a girl,' I said.

MR Crowe in Gladiator

'Of course he does,' said Will. 'That's why he's got a bird's name. So whether you like it or not, by taking this part you are turning yourself into a girl!'

Mel joined in, only she was worse, because girls are just better at saying nasty things and meaning them. Also she'd just broken up with Tarquin after she discovered that he wasn't an actor after all, just the tea boy, who couldn't even make good tea! She hated Pamela as well for getting her part and sneered at her. 'If I'd known they were looking for a dumpy, spotty nine-year-old with greasy hair and no talent I'd never have auditioned,' she said cruelly.

Pamela burst into tears, so I jumped in and defended her honour.

'Shut up, Mel!' I shouted. 'That's not true. She's eleven!'

Richard and Judy have another saying for what happened in the car park:

'Nothing pursues celebrityhood like jealousy and spitefulness.'

How true that is!

Ralph and Aaron turned up after everyone had gone. They'd found the fart cushion, but it had a puncture. Their jaws hit the ground when I told them I'd got the part.

'It's lucky you're going to Spain then,' said Aaron, 'because you can get yourself a tan. That's the first thing a celebrity gets, apart from a drug habit.'

I told them that Mum had said I couldn't be in it, but they said that once she knew that I was on the verge of International Celebrityhood she'd be my rock and sandwich-maker.

'And clothes-washer too,' said Ralph. 'All those white suits are going to take some sponging.'

'Harry Potter's mum must do tons of stuff like that,' said Aaron. 'He's made three films now.'

'Harry Potter's not real,' laughed Ralph.

'He is,' said Aaron. 'I've seen him.'

'It's an actor. Harry's made up.'

'That's because he's in films,' said Aaron. 'All actors wear make-up.'

'I am not turning into a girl!' I shouted.

'Who said you were?' said Ralph. 'Can I be your manager?'

Wish you were here, instead of me! A.

Fellow Revengers secret address
Tooting

Happiness is an emotion I know nothing about. Examine this: for the first time in my miserable life I was HAPPY discussing my jet-set future with the Revengers. I was ENJOYING my last walk home without dark glasses. But an evil spirit must have known this and rung ahead, because as I turned the corner of my street this HAPPINESS was brutally snatched away from me and I was plunged into a vicious spiral of loathing and revenge. Why? Because parked in our drive, with a mushroom for a chimneypot and a windowbox full of plastic flowers, was an off-white box on wheels, more commonly known as a caravan.

This should be the dictionary definition of a caravan:

CARAVAN/kaere,vaen/(n.) − 1. A tiny mobile home with only one loo which means you have to smell other people's socks and farts all day, which holds up the traffic and makes you a laughing stock if you're seen in it. 2. A wrecker of dreams when your mum announces that she has cancelled your holiday to Spain and is taking you on a caravan tour of England instead, to find interesting local recipes from interesting locals to put in her stupid new TV series and book called Towed in the Hole! 3. A good motive for murder. Especially when your mum's rubbish idea is messing up your brilliant plans to be a dead famous film star!

The rest of today's diary has been cancelled as a mark of respect for the end of my life and the death of my one chance to make a celebrity out of myself.

RIP = not Rest In Peace, you sillykins.
RIP = Revenge Is planned!

R.I.P

ALISTAIR FURY

NO ONE SPECIAL.
JUST A BORING
ORDINARY BLOKE LIKE
EVERYONE ELSE IN THE
WORLD. HE HAD ONE
CHANCE TO FLY TO THE
STARS BUT HIS MOTHER
BROKE HIS WINGS.

THANKS, MUM.

Woke from horrible nightmare to discover it was all true. This is what happened last night.

Mum announced cancellation of Spanish holiday in favour of caravan trip around England. TV producer, Michael, will try to sell idea of *Towed in the Hole!* to BBC,

while Mum finds local dishes, and dishy locals who cook them, to put in the show.

Announcement met with howls of dismay. William hated Spain, but hated caravans even more. Mel stamped her big foot and screamed at Mum to pay back all the money she'd spent on clothes for Spain.

'And in case you hadn't noticed, I'm single and lonely again! Which means I need to ring boys on my mobile all the time. How can I make private calls in a pooey caravan the size of a bird house! And if I don't meet a new boyfriend my life will be over and I'll end up a disgusting old spinster with a moustache!'

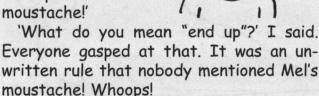

'What do you mean "end up"?' I said. Everyone gasped at that. It was an unwritten rule that nobody mentioned Mel's moustache! Whoops!

Dad was happy going to Spain, because it was a place where criminals could go to escape the long arm of the law, but a trip round England – *No!* He'd be recognized on the streets and arrested. Only Granny Constance fancied a tour in a caravan.

'I'll bring my Travel Scrabble,' she said, 'with the Grip-Master tiles in case we hit any potholes. And I can look after the pets while you taste the local food, Celia. I won't be any trouble. I'll bring three packets of laxative to make sure. Holidays always play havoc with my bowels.' This was more information than any living being needed.

Later, Mel slammed the front door as she left the house in search of Boyfriend Number 1034. She had a freshly bleached moustache that made her look like an albino walrus.

But Mum was not going to budge. We were leaving in two days' time for a fort-night and that was that! That was *not* that! That was right across my film shoot next weekend!

Applause & dramatic music fades as Alistair Fury accepts Oscar from Dame Denise van Outen.

ALISTAIR FURY (*gushing tears*): Thank you, thank you, thank you. This is incredible. Think of all the wonderful actors who've

68

been trying to be famous all their lives and have never won *any* award, let alone an Oscar. And this is my first film. (*He blushes modestly*) Gosh, I must either be extremely lucky or exceptionally good – and I'm never lucky! I'd like to thank my mother for helping to launch my career and being so supportive. I'd like to, but I can't. The truth is she did everything in her power to stop me from becoming an actor and I'd be lying if I said I was sorry at the tragic accident that ended her life yesterday, when a man in a baboon costume jumped out of a hole in the road and kicked her into a sewer.

Aaron said I should just *not go* on caravan holiday. Nobody ever noticed me when I was there, so they wouldn't miss me if I wasn't. Ralph had a different plan. If I *did* have to go he could take my part in the film. I suspected he was trying to steal my celebrity ticket and nick the fame that

was mine by rights on account of my huge talent. This wasn't going to happen. Just in case, told Ralph that I would curse him and his children and their children, and all of their cousins as well, to everlasting seaweed hair (that's hair made from sea-weed and held on by the sucking power of barnacles) if he so much as whispered a single line from my part under his breath. So far, seaweed bluff is holding up.

Mum spent evening planning caravan route on computer, leaving Dad and me to play Scrabble with Granny. Mood of house reflected in words on board methinks. HATE, ENEMY, NO, WON'T, DIVORCE, SPARE and ROOM. Plus BOWELS, CRAMP, STRAIN, PAIN and BLOCKAGE. The last lot were Granny's.

Mel came home happy, because she had just met a new boyfriend called Rodney.

'I think I know him,' I said. 'Is he that blind man who likes the taste of bleach when he kisses?' For that, I

BOYFRIEND NO 125,796

this week!

my dead Leg

got a dead leg, which I vowed never to forget. Then Miss Moustachio went upstairs to text the life out of Rodney and I went to bed cursing my mum and her stupid stupid stupid stupid stupid stupid job!

That all happened last night. It is now Sunday and I have one day left to save my film career before Mum wrecks my life and condemns me to the obscurity of a dull job spraying Day-Glo paint round holes in the pavement.

Called emergency Revenger meeting at 12 p.m. to discuss emergency revenges. I am tearing up all previous revenge plans and starting again. Feel tense. What I need is a relaxing bath.

Can't use bathroom as Mel has moved in and is txting her new boyfriend. More tense now than ever before.

'You've been in there three hours!' I shouted through door. 'How much more is there to tell him about your life?'

'I'm up to what present I got given on my fourth birth-day,' she said.

'But I'm desperate!' I howled.

'Tough!' she said. 'You should have thought of that before you accepted the part.'

Will was delighted that the bathroom was occupied. 'I hate brushing my teeth,' he said.

'You don't say,' I said, using Mum's hairdryer to blow his bad breath out of my face.

'I can't wait till I'm eighteen,' he mumbled, 'because then I can stop washing altogether.'

IMPORTANT MEMO TO SELF
BE in australia ON
William's 18th birthday.

Breakfast – Dad still wearing dark glasses. He spent night forging new driving licence in name of Sean Pury. The man is a genius.

The only member of the police force who is going to be fooled by an inked-over F is a police dog!

Letter arrived from director confirming that I would start a week today. Read it secretly under table so traitor couldn't read it over my shoulder. She was on phone anyway, to Michael. He told her to keep her mobile near her at all times in case a big cheese from the BBC wanted a

Hi, I'm from the BBC

word about the format of *Towed in the Hole!*

The PS on my letter read:

```
'Before you arrive
    next Sunday
   please take
dancing lessons.'
```

Went upstairs and phoned Mrs Muttley. Asked her if she could dance. She ignored my question. 'The director hasn't phoned,' she said accusingly. 'What did you tell him?'

'How lovely and fragrant you were,' I said, reading the words off an air-freshener can that Granny had left outside Will's bedroom door. 'A real breath of fresh air who gets to work on whiffs.'

'Come along in an hour,' she said. 'I'll try to get hold of Pamela. And bring a leotard.'

Leotard? Where was I going to find a big cat breeder in Tooting? Looked up word in my dictionary and saw what it meant. Found stretchy one-piece in Mum's wardrobe from when she was young and could still take exercise. Borrowed that.

Met Mel coming out of bathroom.

'Still jealous?' I said.

'Still need a pee?' she retorted.

'No,' I said, 'I went in your shoes.'

'Then I'm not jealous,' she replied. 'I know I'm a better actor than you, Alice. It's just that director. He's an idiot.'

made Mel's shoes smell nicer !!

'He speaks very highly of you,' I said. 'Although he did pass some comment about your acting being wooden!'

'Good,' she said hysterically. 'Good! Because wooden is good! Let's see who's the best at wooden, shall we? We'll both pretend to be a tree and whoever's the best wins.'

'That's stupid,' I said. 'Who's going to judge who's the best tree?'

'Mr E,' she said. 'If he pees up your leg, you win!'

MR E! MR E! OH MY GOD, MR E!

Luckily the high-sided skip had not been collected from the car park. When I found Mr E, he was asleep in an old picnic hamper covered in fish heads, potato peelings, half a bucket of congealed chip fat, some mouldy cabbage leaves and a particularly unpleasant quilt of green snot! He smelled rather fresher than usual. And when I got him home he wasn't hungry either. Must have eaten already. Probably that nappy he was using as a pillow.

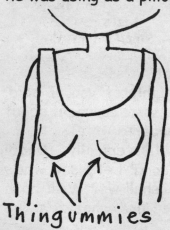

Thingummies

Got to Mrs Muttley's just after Pamela Whitby. Her leotard was brand new. It didn't look anything like mine. Hers had legs and arms, where mine had cups for Mum's thingummies.

'Why are you wearing a woman's bathing costume?' asked Pamela. 'Are you really a girl, Alistair?'

'No,' I said, 'I'm not.'

'Is that why you do dancing, because you wish you were a girl?'

'I'm not a girl!' I cried.

'No,' she said. 'You're one of the most

miserable people I've ever met. If you were a dog my father would take you out and shoot you.'

'But he's not a dog,' said Mrs Muttley. 'He's a leaping impala. Shall we dance?'

After half an hour of being a flat-footed antelope the lesson, mercifully, came to an end. Mrs Muttley kept wanting me to lift Pamela up by putting my arms around her waist, but Pamela wouldn't let me. Every time I tried it she slapped my face. My cheeks hurt so much I had to make up an excuse why I couldn't do it any more.

'I'm not muscly enough to lift a whole person,' I said feebly.

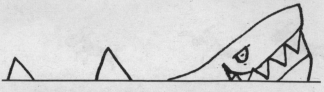

'Nonsense,' said Mrs Muttley. 'Again!'

I let Pamela fall to prove my point.

After Pamela had been carted off to hospital to have her knees X-rayed, I asked Mrs Muttley if there was any way she could get the director to move his dates until after my caravan holiday. She said she didn't think so. She showed me a letter that had arrived from the director ten minutes after our phone call.

Dear Mrs Muttley,

You and me? A couple? Ha ha ha ha ha ha ha ha ha ha ha ha ha ha ha ha ha ha ha ha ha ha ha ha ha ha ha ha ha ha ha ha ha ha ha ha ha ha ha ha ha ha ha ha ha ha ha ha ha ha ha ha ha ha ha ha ha ha ha ha ha ha ha ha ha ha ha ha ha ha ha!

The Director

P.S - Ha ha ha ha ha ha ha ha ha ha ha ha ha ha ha ha ha ha ha ha ha ha ha ha ha ha ha ha ha ha ha ha ha ha ha ha ha ha ha ha ha ha ha ha ha ha ha ha ha ha ha ha ha ha ha ha ha ha ha ha ha ha ha ha ha ha ha!

'Do you think he likes me?' she asked.

12 p.m. – I had called the emergency Revenger meeting *in* the caravan so that we could get to know our enemy. Our enemy has very plastic seats that stick to the backs of your thighs.

It was Ralph's fault that meeting was a disaster. He'd bought two webcams for him and Aaron, so that we could stay in touch while we were on holiday in different places. He'd also brought his mobile and laptop with him, and Aaron had his mum's. My mum was using her laptop to print out detailed directions for every day of our caravan journey into hell. So I unplugged it. And stole her mobile. Then we attached the three webcams to the three computers, and linked the computers through our mobile phones.

'What a palaver,' I said. 'Why don't we just phone each other? It'd be much simpler.'

'But not as much fun,' said Ralph. He was right. We chatted for hours with our faces on the screens, doing really funny stuff like:

'Apollo whatever to Earth - **BEEP** - Am going for landing on moon - **BEEP**-'

'Be careful, Chunky Baldrin - **BEEP** - There may be **aliens** - **BEEP**-'

'It's OK - **BEEP** - I've seen David Dickinson - **BEEP** - Nothing can scare me any more - **BEEP**-'

'And stop saying **BEEP**, you stupid **BEEP**.'

'You started it, you fat **BEEP** with a goldfish bowl for a head! Go **BEEP** in your spacesuit, and shove your **BEEP** up your skinny **BEEP** until **BEEP** whis-

tIes Dixie on your big fat BEEP.
BEEP!'

oops...beep

pnft

Oh, how we laughed!

That was when the door burst open and Mel barged in with her new boyfriend, Rodney. They needed somewhere private to practise their txting apparently.

'Oh yeah!' I sneered. 'Pull the other one. Don't you mean sxting?'

They threw us out into the shivering cold. Now we didn't have anywhere to meet. To pay the DIRTYLUVBIRDS back we stuffed the hosepipe up the chemical loo. The idea was to switch it on and backflush the contents all over the floor while they were snogging. We hoped they'd dissolve in the chemicals! But when we pushed the hose up the loo pipe there was a Rodney-type scream and before we could switch the tap on Rodney had counter-attacked by flushing the loo. Bright blue sticky stuff shot out of the hosepipe and covered us.

Mum had to wash our clothes before they burned our skin, so Ralph and Aaron were allowed to stay the night. I was glad. I was still going on helliday in the morning and this gave us extra hours to think about the following important things thoroughly.

THE FOLLOWING THINGS WHICH WE THOUGHT ABOUT THOROUGHLYish

A. was MOST IMPORTANT as it affected me being a celebrity. How to wreck the caravan holiday so that I could get back home in time for filming next week.
B. How to stuff Will and Mel for being so horrible to me especially now, but all my life generally.

C. How to pay Mum back for not letting me do film, killing the creative flame within and butchering my career.
D. How to avoid being the one who has to play Scrabble with Granny all day and every day.

Because I will not be seeing the Revengers for weeks, I have written the revenges down. This way I will not forget them.

IDEAS TO GET OUT OF CARAVAN HOLIDAY

1. Give myself a black eye and blame it on Will and Mel. Then say that I am too scared and/or septic to go on holiday with big brother and sister, and will stay at home instead while everyone goes without me.

Agreed that Ralph and Aaron would hit me in the eyes, but neither wanted to do it. Decided that they would leave it till a time of their choosing when they would just surprise me.

83

2. Secondly, curries and farts, carsickness, nosepicking and snorting back really big gobbets of snot. Anything really to make me repulsive-to-be-close-to, so that Mum and Dad would turn the car round and come home.

HUGE BIG SNOT GOBBET →

3. Thirdly, change Mum's route plan to send us in wrong direction. She'd get lost, give up and come home.

4. Fourthly, invent a stalker to scare Mum rigid. Then tell her that she would only be

WELCOME TO BEING LOST YOU ARE HERE →

safe AT HOME and make it convincing.

5. Fifthly, scatter woodland creatures in and around the caravan. Then contact the World Wildlife Foundation and get them to declare the caravan a place of out-standing natural beauty, which must stay EXACTLY WHERE IT IS and not move an inch. (NB – Caravan already has precious collection of toadstools in kitchen.)

6. Sixthly, when we are parked up at night in layby, surround caravan with cardboard cut-out figures of life-sized braves on mustangs. Then shout, 'Indians at twelve o'clock! And nine! And three! And eleven

thirty!' Whip up sense of panic and insist that we go home before they scalp us and wear our ears as moccasins. (NB – Will not work in day as Mum will see that Indian braves & horses are cut out of cereal packets.)

9.30 p.m. – I loved the woodland creatures idea, because it meant the caravan wouldn't even leave home. But finding woodpeckers, shrews, miniature voles and badgers at nine o'clock at night in Tooting is no easy task. Plus the World Wildlife Foundation only save creatures between 9 a.m. and 5 p.m., Monday to Friday. We know because Aaron phoned them up and got an answer-phone.

9.35 p.m. – Should have put Mum's computer back ages ago, but just had a brilliant idea to pay back big brother and sister.

'We send an e-mail to someone famous from Will and Mel,' I said. 'Only it's not a nice e-mail, it's rude! And we get them into big big trouble.' The obvious question was who did we send it to?

'We don't know the addresses of any famous people,' said Ralph.

Aaron laughed like he couldn't believe his luck. 'I know one,' he said. 'It was on a petition my mum signed.'

STUFFING UP WILL AND MEL

Using Mum's computer we dialled up the President of the United States of America on *president@whitehouse.com* and left the following e-mail.

America sucks!
We think you stink!
Love Melanie & William Fury
(Melanie's Mobile – 08775 162 432)

If that didn't get them into deep poo we didn't know what would. With any luck the CIA and FBI would DTI!

Sometimes, when one thinks of a genius

87

idea it's like composing a great symphony or writing a novel or painting the roof of the Sistine Chapel. People often forget that Revenge is an art form that could easily be talked about in coffee bars if only the public would JUST SHOW AN INTEREST! For instance, I know that God is jealous that he never thought of some of the things that I've thought of. He's stuck in a rut with his 'tooth for a tooth and eye for an eye'. That guy needs fresh ideas.

10.55 p.m. - Ran out of time to plan proper revenges for C & D. Mum is screaming for lights out as I have early start tomorrow. Made pact with Revengers that wherever we might be in the world over the next few weeks, we would link up via webcams for daily updates every night at 8 o'clock.

10.59 p.m. – Returned Mum's computer and mobile phone. Instead of pressing RESUME PRINTING straight away, we made a few tiny changes to her directions first. We changed Lefts for Rights, Norths for Souths, Dead Ends for Dual Carriageways and Traffic Lights for Roundabouts. All those hours she spent writing out road directions in easy-to-follow lists – so tragically wasted!

11.28 p.m. – Just before lights out, Aaron and Ralph leaned across and said, 'Good night, Alistair. Have a happy holiday.' Then they punched me in one eye each.

'Thanks,' I said. 'I won't.'

MONDAY (DAY 3)

Woke up to rain. Hoorah! ——————→ Sarcastic

That should make the caravanning experience even more cold, wet and unappealing. Rushed to mirror to check eyes. Hoorah! ——————————————→ Genuine

Both eyes had black rings around them. Turned on waterworks and quivering, brave-little-soldier bottom lip, then ran downstairs to show Mum.

'Look what Will and Mel have done to me!' I trembled. 'Oh, Mummy, I can't go on holiday with my big brother and sister now, because I am so frightened of what they might do to me in the back of the car.'

'You're still coming,' she said, wrapping sandwiches in cling film. 'Hurry up. We're leaving in half an hour.'

'I think he should stay,' said Dad, lowering his newspaper and peering over his dark glasses. 'He'll have to cover up those black eyes and if two of us are wearing dark glasses in the car then the police will stop us, thinking we're Mafia.'

'*You're* not wriggling out of it either,' snarled Mum.

'But Celia, what's going to happen to this family when I'm banged up in prison?'

'We'll have lower electricity bills,' Mum said sweetly, 'because the TV will be *off* sometimes.'

'We'll fall apart,' cried Dad. 'I do everything round this house.'

'That's right,' smiled Mum. 'Everything except clean, wash, cook, shop, sew, paint, make the beds and pay the bills.'

It was always like this. I would start a conversation, everyone else would join in and before very long I would be forgotten.

'Excuse me,' I said. 'But I'm the one who's been beaten up here!'

'Nasty eyes,' said Mel, entering the room with Will. 'I think Alice should stay here and I'll stay with him to be his nurse.'

Why did everyone have to interfere with my plan? They always over-complicated things.

'No!' I screamed. 'She's just saying that to stay with her boring boyfriend. Anyway, it can't be Mel who stays, she did this to me, she wants to murder me!'

'I do now,' she hissed. Then loudly, 'I did not do that to him!'

'Ma knee!' grunted William.

'What's wrong with it?' said Mum.

'No!' wailed Will. 'Ma knee, ma knee, ma knee!'

'I think what Our Son the Primate is trying to say,' said Dad, 'is "Me neither". He didn't hurt Alistair either.'

'Oh really,' I said in my most injured voice. 'So I just punched *myself* in the face, I suppose.'

'Probably,' said Dad. 'You're mad enough.'

And so it went on until Mum blew a whistle.

'We're all going,' she said. 'And that's that.'

'Even us?' asked Ralph and Aaron, who

Dad included

had come down for breakfast.

'No,' said Mum. 'Not you!'

I saw one last chink in her armour. 'Oh but that's not fair!' I howled. 'You always let Ralph and Aaron do what they want and never me!'

Everyone stopped and stared at me.

'We're guests,' said Ralph. 'Guests always get what they want.'

'That's right,' said Mum.

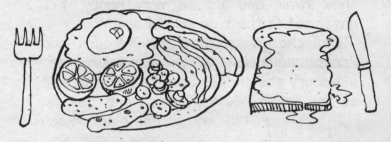

So Ralph and Aaron asked for bacon, sausage, two tomatoes, mushrooms, poached eggs and some thick white buttered toast. Mum said no.

Then she lined us up in the hall and said, 'I am fed up trying to be enthusiastic for everyone in this family. I only do the hard work that I do for you lot, so that you can go to a nice school wearing nice clothes and eat nice food.'

'But we don't eat nice food,' I said. 'We have to eat the muck what you cook, like Sautéed Snails and Cold Chameleon Tongue and Houlash of Horse's Heart!

Plus, William's clothes aren't nice at all, they stink, and I'd be very happy if I never set foot inside school again!'

Got chased upstairs with Mason and Pearson hairbrush. When Mum is only act-ing-angry she chases us with the flat side of the brush – lots of swish and thwack,

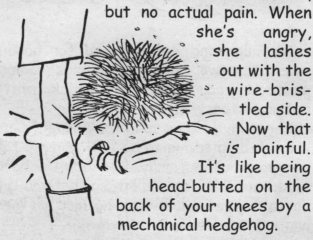

but no actual pain. When she's angry, she lashes out with the wire-bris-tled side. Now that *is* painful. It's like being head-butted on the back of your knees by a mechanical hedgehog.

Did not take this heartless, unprovoked beating from cruel slave-mother lying down. I couldn't – my bum was stinging too much. So I *stood up* and exacted my revenge. While William refused to pack a bag because he hated clothes, and Mel dragged her sixteenth suitcase down the stairs, causing Mum's sixteenth shout of: 'For goodness' sake, Melanie, this isn't a fashion parade. We're only going for two weeks!' I stood by freezer and ate every tub of ice cream I could find. In my stomach I had a mixture of chocolate chips, sticky toffee, pecans, walnuts, marshmallows, fudge brownies, cookie-dough, vanilla pods, fresh strawberries, raspberry ripple, caramel chews, lemon zest, jelly beans, meringue bits, brown bread, violet creams, bananas, maple syrup, rum, raisins, lamb chops and chives.

I was like an ice-cream time bomb waiting to explode!

This last flavour was Mum's invention.

95

It was time to go. I could tell because nobody was anywhere near the car or the caravan and Mum had been calling for us until she was blue in the face. Then she went red. Then purple. Then violet with crimson blotches.

'Your face is a funny colour,' I told her, as I sauntered out of the front door. 'You should see a doctor. Tell you what – why don't you have some tests and I'll wait at home for two weeks for the results? It's all right, you don't have to thank me.' Nice try, but Mum wasn't buying it.

Granny turned up with a steamer trunk. Suspect it's called that because it's big enough to lie inside and have a sauna in. She was quite put out when Mum said she'd be more comfy in the caravan with the pets.

'Whatever you want, Celia,' she said, biting her lip. 'If I'm tossed around and my fragile skull is smashed to pieces like a Ming vase in a hurricane, so be it. I said I'd look after the pets, and look after them I will. I don't mind travelling Animal Class. Just remember I'm back here when we stop to eat though. I *could* live off the toadstools growing on the wallpaper but

I'd prefer not to.' Then she read out her strict Rules for Caravanning.

Granny Constance's Strict Rules For Caravanning

1. Who has toilet first is always decided on basis of Age before Beauty. First Come First Served will not wash in this caravan.

2. Toilet Paper is a precious commodity and will be rationed and allocated on basis of Age before Beauty.

3. Exemptions from duties on Daily Rota (see separate sheet) will be decided on basis of Age before Beauty.

4. Anything that needs to be done and involves a bit of work will be allocated on basis of Beauty before Age.

5. No swearing.

6. No snoring.

7. No sniggering behind Granny's back.

8. No excuses to be made for not playing Scrabble.

9. No signalling the enemy with Venetian blinds and an oil lamp.

I asked Granny if she'd done a lot of caravanning before.

'Never,' she said. 'But I lived through the Blitz and that was horrible too.'

She pinned rota onto back of cupboard door in caravan's kitchen. This is what it looked like when she put it up.

THE ROTA

Key

GC = Granny Constance
D = Dad
M = Mum
ML = Mel
W = William
A = Alistair

	DAY 1	DAY 2	DAY 3	DAY 4	DAY 5	DAY 6	DAY 7
CLEANING	ML	W	A	M	D	ML	W
IRONING	W	A	M	D	ML	W	A
WASHING UP	A	M	D	ML	W	A	M
COOKING	M	D	ML	W	A	M	D
MAKING BEDS	D	ML	W	A	M	D	ML

This is what it looked like three minutes later.

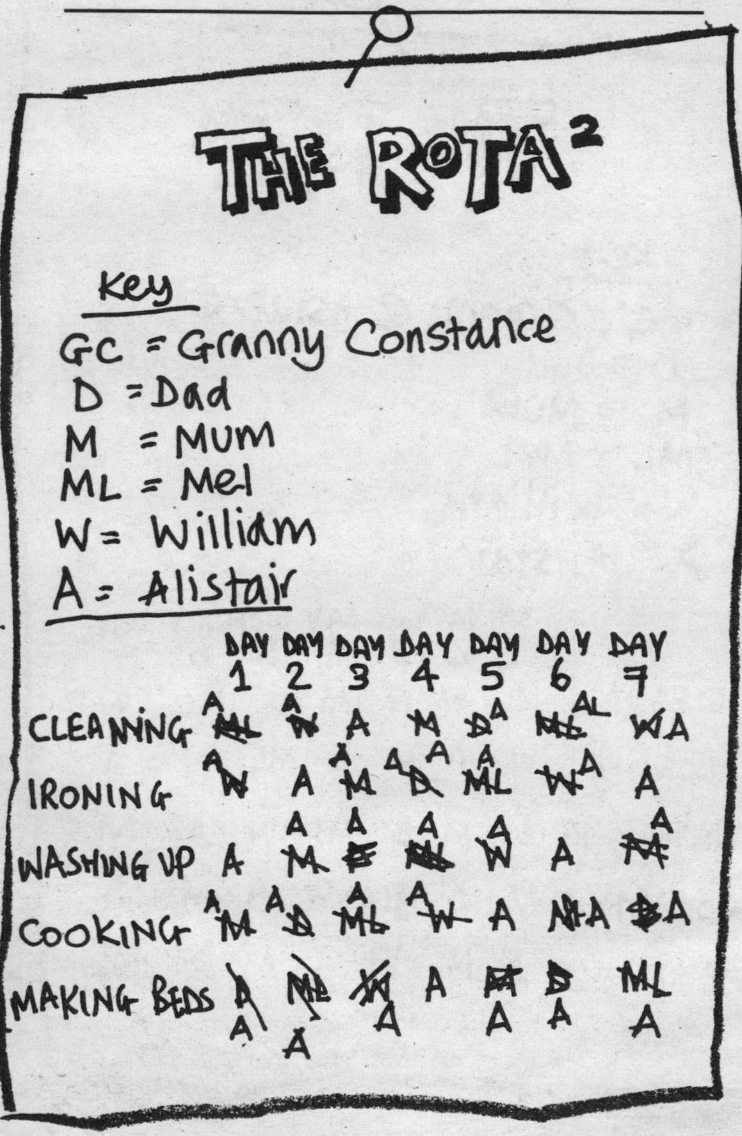

THE ROTA²

Key

GC = Granny Constance
D = Dad
M = Mum
ML = Mel
W = William
A = Alistair

	DAY 1	DAY 2	DAY 3	DAY 4	DAY 5	DAY 6	DAY 7
CLEANING	ML A	W	A	M	D A	ML AL	W A
IRONING	W A	A	M A	D A	ML	W A	A
WASHING UP	A	M A	A	ML A	W A	A	M A
COOKING	M A	D A	ML A	W A	A	M A	D A
MAKING BEDS	A A	ML A	W A	A	M A	D A	ML A

And this is what it looked like three minutes after that.

Little wonder that I am twisted and bitter. My life is like a Hoover. It sucks in many different ways, and never gives anything back.

On front lawn, Ralph and Aaron encouraged me to do a war dance, so that ice-cream shake was nicely blended when Mum announced our departure for the sixty-fourth time. I was still jumping up and down when Dad rushed out and ducked down behind every bush between front door and car. He was camouflaging himself in case the police had helicopters. Just as I was told to get in the car, I felt my stomach clench.

'Oh Mummy,' I cried. 'You're never going to believe this, but I don't feel well.' She didn't believe it. I could tell by that look on her face. Privately, I call it her 'Meet Your Foster Parents' face. 'I can't go. Sorry. I think I need my bed—' Then I spewed a warm ice-cream puddle all over the grass, which Mr E lapped up in seconds flat. He loved it. Mum should branch out into pet food. She could market my sick as Bow-Wow Baked Alaska.

As first nutty chunks hit the ground,

Trust me, we had to board up this picture – you REALLY don't want to see it.

Dad, Mel and Will jumped straight out of the car and headed indoors.

'Oh dear!' they said unconvincingly. 'We can't possibly go now if Alice is ill. We're staying.'

I thought we were going to win, but Mum said, 'Take one more step, any of you, and I'll reverse the caravan over your legs!' Which pretty much summed up how much this holiday meant to her.

Actually that's what happened. Aaron and Ralph said they'd help Dad reverse the caravan out onto the road. But caravans turn the opposite way to the steering wheel and Dad was too thick to work it out. He said it was very confusing, like patting your head and rubbing your stomach at the same time.

'I can do that,' Will said to me. 'I can pat your head while you're rubbing your stomach.' Then he punched me in the stomach and while I was rubbing it better he belted me round the head.

103

Actually it was Ralph's, but he said I could say it was mine if it made me happy. Which it does.

Then he leaned over the back of Dad's seat and put his Death Metal CD into the CD player. The noise was deafening – at least that was Dad's excuse for what happened next. As he tried to steer the caravan through the gates, he ran over Aaron's foot. The neighbours saw Aaron crying and called the police. When Dad saw the police car he legged it into the caravan to hide, leaving Mum in the car to take the rap. It was then that I had my stonking idea!

MY STONKING IDEA!

If I told the police it was Dad who was driving and they arrested him and then found out that he was the Most Wanted Man in Britain for skipping Jury Service, he'd go down for several years. Mum could hardly take us on a caravan holiday while Dad's freedom was at stake! So I shopped him.

The police found Dad hiding under Granny's sofa in the caravan. They pulled

him out by his ankles and frowned. Dad smiled and made up some cheesy excuse like: 'Oh hello, officer, I wasn't hiding. I was checking under the sofa panels for rats. Seems OK now, actually. I can go and sit back down in the passenger seat and let my wife continue driving us to our lovely holiday destination. Excuse me.'

'So why are you holding a tea towel over your face, sir?'

'Am I?' laughed Dad. 'I didn't notice. I'm not hiding behind it. I'm not. I sometimes read the washing labels on tea towels. Maybe it was that. Oh look, one hundred per cent cotton. Hmm, fascinating.'

The officer asked to see Dad's driving licence. 'I see, sir, so your name's Sean Pury, is it?'

'Ah . . .'

'I'll pretend I'm not looking at this, sir, because if I was *you'd* be looking at fifteen years for forgery.'

Dad showed his real license and offered another pathetic excuse. 'That licence,' he said, 'the Sean Pury one, got put in the wash by mistake and the ink must have run.'

Dad got a £60 on-the-spot fine and was allowed to go. Can you believe that?

WHAT IS WRONG WITH OUR POLICE FORCE?

Instead of spending all their days catching criminals, the police should spend more time banging up my family on trumped-up charges, so that I can live my life the way I want to. I know I don't pay any taxes, but do I not have rights too? Do I not have the right to be a famous film star with flash cars and lovely ladies if I want to? I think I do. And it's the police's duty to keep my family off my back so that I can exercise this right. Honestly, I some-times despair at the state of this country!

Dad sat in the driver's seat weeping with the shame of nearly being a criminal, while I was ostracized for grassing up my own father. Mel and Will tied me up in the seat belts on the back seat and poked my ribs till I was sore.

'Road's clear,' said Aaron, whose foot was fine again after causing all that bother for nothing.

Dad drove towards M3 like a snail. He couldn't see any-thing out of the back,

because there was a huge great caravan behind him. Thought he might have expected that. Everything I ever thought was embarrassing about caravans *was*. Jeering children on pavements, angry

motorists beeping their horns and calling Dad fruity names, mothers with prams leaping onto zebra crossings to test Dad's brakes. Every time he braked hard the caravan skidded and there was a yelp of pain from inside. It was Granny as she slid through the kitchen and banged her knees on the oven door.

Have some sympathy for me...those knees hurt!!

One hour drifted into the next. Mum read her directions out loud and looked puzzled as we passed the same landmarks three or four times. Mel stared at her mobile phone and rattled it occasionally, putting it to her ear to check it was still working. The car doors vibrated from the noise of Will's music.

Will said he hated roads. 'They just stop you from getting where you want to go!' he moaned. Then he went to sleep with his head on my belted-up shoulder.

The heat from his head and the sliding round corners had a bad effect on my stomach. I thought I'd got everything out on the lawn, but obviously not. I told Dad I was going to be sick, but he couldn't find a long enough parking space to pull into. Then Mel screamed and Dad jumped so badly he nearly hit a hospital. Her mobile phone had stopped working. Then it hadn't. Then it had. Then it hadn't. Then it had. I pointed out that it might have got something to do with the tunnels we were going through. She thumped my arm and said she knew. But she didn't. She shouted at Dad that this was an emergency and he had to pull up at the next mobile phone shop or she'd stop breathing! And then her phone rang.

It was Rodney surprising her with a call. You'd have thought she'd have been happy as that was what she'd been waiting for for the last three hours, but she screamed at Rodney like he was her little brother and told him to USE HIS BRAIN

i.e. MEl

110

Filthy rude, I bet.

and THINK next time he called. She couldn't speak when she was in the car with her family all around eavesdropping, could she? He had to text.

While Mel went all giggly at Rodney's TXTMSG,

Mum and Dad had a fight. The directions she was following were wrong. She couldn't work out why we were driving away from the M3. Dad decided to stick the steering wheel on permanent lock round a roundabout. We went round and round and round and round until they'd sorted where to go. Then he refused to stop until Mum apologized for falsely blaming him for not knowing the way. This circular motion did nothing for my mouth, which was filling up with sicky water.

NOTE OF CAUTION

Sometimes Revenges can backfire.

Mel was making matters worse by staring at me with stupid gooey eyes like I was her baby or something.

'Mum,' I shouted. 'Mel's staring at me.'

'I'm not,' she smirked.

'She is,' I said. 'Tell her to stop.'

'I can look if I want to,' she said. 'Is there a law against it, Alice? I don't think so!'

'Now she's calling me Alice,' I whined. 'Make her stop, Mum. Give her some lines!'

The temperature was rising. Mum was

blaming Dad for driving like a mole and Dad was blaming Mum for being the blind one, because she couldn't read her own directions.

'But how can I tell where we're going if the directions are wrong?' she shouted.

'So,' I said, 'LET'S NOT GO!'

Silence fell like an executioner's axe.

Then Mum screamed. Dad jumped and banged his head on the roof. The caravan slid across the road, bumped up a pavement and hooked onto a bouncy castle that a pair of clowns were blowing up outside a school playground. We were the length of a juggernaut when Dad got us straight on the road – the car followed by the caravan followed by the bouncy castle. And up ahead was another roundabout.

'Oh look!' shouted Mum, pointing to a sign. 'The M3's to the right.'

Dad tried to make the turn, but he was just too long. By the time we ground to a halt there were three cyclists and an

Which wasn't far because there was a caravan and a bouncy castle behind us.

electric wheelchair in the bouncy castle and a traffic jam behind us stretching back as far as we could see.

We could also hear a police siren. And I still hadn't been sick.

I was saving that for when the policewoman opened the driver's door and removed her hat. I did cry, 'Sorry!' so nobody can say I wasn't polite or didn't warn her, but all that bouncy bouncy had churned me up. I filled her hat till it was brimming with multi-coloured minestrone. Then I wiped my mouth on the back of my hand and tried to smile.

'You've got something stuck in your teeth,' she said coldly.

'Is it going to be your fist?' Will asked her excitedly. It was a bit of pecan.

Mum's tissues only went so far. I'd filled up the runners under Dad's seat as well. Dad's precious chamois leather just smeared it across the carpet, so Mum went to get some loo paper from the caravan, only Granny wouldn't let her have any on account of Granny's bowels being a bit unpredictable on holiday. So it was Mr E – or, as I nickname him, Dyson, the Super-sucking Twin-cyclone Dog – who was wheeled in to do the business.

Unfortunately, his little tummy was full before the sick had all gone. I remember the look of disappointment on Mum's face as she stared at me and said,

PUGOOIZ
DOG HOOVER

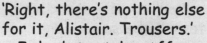

'Right, there's nothing else for it, Alistair. Trousers.'

I had to take off my trousers by the side of the road and stand there being honked at by laughing lorries while Mum used them to wipe up the rest of car and the whole of the WPC. They were my favourites as well, which only goes to prove that Life Is Pants in more ways than one.

Dad got away with a second warning, another £60 fine and a bill for a new hat. If only British police would be a bit more bent, I could have bribed her with a whole pound to lock Dad up and then we could have gone home. Sadly, I only thought of this after she'd driven off to find a dry cleaner's.

I was chucked out of the Chunderbus and shoved in the caravan with Granny. My big brother and sister decided that thirty-six games of Scrabble was worse than the smell of my sick.

Am shocked. Have just played Scrabble with Granny and she used all sorts of REALLY REALLY **REALLY** rude words that I know, obviously, but would never dream of using in front of her. It is a rotten fix and a swindle. If I can't use them, because I'm too young, she shouldn't be allowed to use them either. It's cheating. When I told Granny this she laughed.

'They're not rude words,' she said.

'Well S*** is,' I said.

'No it's not,' she said. 'A s*** means the upper forearm of an organ grinder so it's perfectly all right.'

A p p a r e n t l y, B******* are heavy salamis that a cowboy hangs off his saddle-bags. F****** are vagabonds who invite themselves into your house and clean your windows. And the King is a w***** means that the King is not well respected by his peers.

'What are peers?' I asked her.

'People who pee,' she said.

I hated losing, but I had no idea that Scrabble could be so instructive.

Napoleon had difficulty standing up in the caravan on account of him only having half a tail and even less balance. Every time Dad swung round a corner Napoleon flew across the room like a rock in a spin dryer.

Granny had an idea. 'We're going to make him some catty armour,' she said.

'What's that?' I said.

'They've been making it since the Middle Ages,' she said, 'since cats first went into battle.'

'I didn't know cats fought in battles,' I said.

'You know nothing,' she said. 'You've heard of Dogs of War – terriers who softened up the enemy by nipping their ankles. Well, after the Dogs they used to send in the Cats of War to sit on the enemy's laps and distract them with purring, while the goodies attacked and won.' Then she ordered me to wrap Napoleon in bubble wrap to protect him from the bashes.

'Will you hold him?' I asked.

'No,' she said. 'I can't.'

'Bowels?' I said, knowing that this was

Clever title! The pounds are money pounds, not pounds of weight!

Granny's excuse for getting out of everything.

'No, I don't want to get scratched,' she said. So I got scratched instead.

I made sure I wasn't scratched on the face though. As a shortly-to-be-great-actor my good looks are my passport to celebrityhood. Without my face I am just another ugly extra in the crowd. Taking a leaf out of Richard and Judy's excellent book entitled *How to Gain Pounds and Still Be a Celebrity,*

I wore a saucepan over my head.

'For handling cats always keep a saucepan handy. It can protect your looks and in an emergency can be used to kill the cat with a swift, but humane blow'
(Richard & Judy)

Have always suspected that Mum's new book and series *Towed in the Hole!* was a rubbish idea. This was confirmed when we

120

pulled in at first eatery on gourmet tour – the Grease and Bucket Service Station somewhere bang in the middle of Nowhere Disgusting. We went inside to see what local delights they had on offer.

First on offer – inhospitality. When we walked in, every diner picked up his beer-gut and moved as far away from us as possible. It might have been the smell of sick, because they chucked their knives and forks at us and chanted, 'Kill the sickies! Kill the sickies!' Then the owner pointed to a sign that said NO PETS. So Granny had to leave with Mr E and bubble-wrapped Napoleon.

'Don't worry about me, Celia, I'll be fine in the caravan on my own.'

'Don't be silly,' said Mum. 'You're allowed to eat, Constance.'

'Really?' said Granny. 'But that would just make me live longer, and no one around here wants that, do they?' She left in silence.

Then Dad tried to break the ice with a joke. 'I thought that sign meant you don't *eat* pets in here,' he said. Bad mistake. They clearly *did* eat pets in there.

'Can we go?' I asked.

'No. We came in for food and food is what we're going to get,' hissed Mum. It was turning into a very bad Western.

We ordered the house special and Mum told the owner/chef who she was, but he'd never heard of her. So she sat down looking cross. The meal arrived. It was Spit Roast Chicken. The weird, cross-eyed locals giggled behind their tattoos when we started to eat it.

Then suddenly Mel shrieked and leaped up from the table, bashing her clothes, slapping her face and knocking over the tables next to us. Food went everywhere. There was a wasp on the window. She wouldn't sit down again and went and joined Granny in the caravan, leaving us to defend ourselves against marauding simpletons who demanded money with teaspoons. Two good things came of this:

1. It cost Dad a shed load of cash to pay off the truckers for their wrecked meals. With the two police fines it was turning out to be an expensive holiday. That'll teach the parents!
2. Have found Mel's weakness. Wasps! Stole small pot of honey off table while Mel was dancing around, flapping her clothes and showing all the hairy men her bra strap.

As we were leaving Mum asked for the recipe of the Spit Roast Chicken.

'Why?' said the owner, scratching his one good ear.

'I might want to put it in my programme,' she said.

'B******* you will!' shouted the owner.

'I know what those are!' I cried. 'They're salamis that cowboys hang from their saddlebags.' Everyone looked at me like I was soft in the head.

'But if you really want to know the special ingredient in my Spit Roast Chicken,' grinned the owner, 'it was spit!'

For some reason William found this funny.

So did the truckers. Howls of laughter pursued us out of the café. We walked out with dignity as far as the car park, then legged it to the bushes, where Mum and Dad were sick. I felt like joining them, but didn't have anything left to bring up.

We still had to drive on to our first camp-site, but it was already dark and Dad didn't trust Mum's directions.

'You'll still be trying to find your way out of this car park in the morning!'

'Not true,' she sneered, 'because you'll still be trying to reverse the caravan out of this parking space!'

Then I said, in a mocking way that made them both feel about one inch tall, 'I don't know why you're arguing. I thought one of the joys of caravanning was that you could stop and sleep anywhere.'

We slept in the car park next to the lorries – *Ooooh! Mucho sophisticato!*

Left car windows open to get rid of sick smell and all slept in caravan. Actually I thought smell was worse in here thanks to William's feet, armpits, bottom and mouth.

'You smell like a damp cellar,' I told him.

'It's better than regurgitated chunks,' he replied. My comment was wittier.

8.00 p.m. – Snuck out of caravan with Mum's computer to use her mobile to webcam

Revengers as promised. Disaster! Mel had beaten me to it.

'PUSHOFFALICE, IMTXTING.'

Now I am all alone with no back-up to help me plan revenges. I will never get back for filming. It's true what they say about the loneliness of the long distance revenger. It's lonely.

← lonely revenger (ME!!.)

Then I had a big piece of luck. Mum came out of the caravan to fetch her mobile phone from the car and found Mel using it! I prayed that my big sister would get her head kicked in for being naughty, but girls NEVER get treated like boys. Mums let girls off everything, whereas with boys mums are like monster trucks with huge tractor wheels that drive over you and crush you nearly to death.

'But I had to call Rodney!' Mel cried. 'And my phone isn't working! It hasn't got a signal!'

She only calls Mum 'Mummy' when she wants something she knows she can't have. It's the same with 'I do love you, Mummy' and 'fank yous, Mumsy-poos'. If I write any more of these I shall be sick again.

'You know how important that phone is to me!' shouted Mum. 'It's my lifeline to Michael and the BBC! Its precious battery juice holds our future in its hands!'

Then, just when I felt a Mason and Pearson moment coming on for big sister, Mel put on her poor-little-me face and started to cry. 'But I love him, Mummy. And I have to hear his voice or I cry myself to sleep. Can we go to the mobile phone shop tomorrow to buy me a new phone? Please, Mummy. Can we? Pleeeeeeease!'

'It's not the phone,' I said. 'There's no signal. We're in the country. And we *don't have time* to go shopping!' The quicker we finished Mum's tour, the sooner I'd get home to my film. But this was Mel crying and Mel always got what she wanted.

'Oh, all right,' said Mum, calming down. 'Come here.' Then she hugged Miss Moustachio and while Mel had her head on Mum's shoulder, she stuck her tongue out at me. There is only one word I would say to Mel now . . . **Wasp!**

FANTASIES IN AN IDEAL WORLD

While she's sleeping, I cover Mel's face in rubber. Then I make a mask, which I wear so that I look like Mel. Then I put two grapes in my shirt for boobs and hey

This does not mean I want to be a girl! Ok?

presto, I *am* Mel. And Mum gives me everything I want, because suddenly I'm her favourite!

10.15 p.m. – Back in the caravan, sleeping was impossible. For a start I kept thinking I could hear Mum and Dad kissing. And then I thought I could hear them doing other stuff too, which is really disturbing when you're

disturbed

eleven and delicate. But they weren't because I asked them. Dad had lost his hearing aid under the duvet.

And Granny made more trips to the loo than the whole British Army when they had Delhi Belly.

'The loo's out of bounds to anyone but me,' she announced as we were climbing across each other to get into bed. 'It's not my fault I'm a slave to my bowels.' It wasn't ours either, but we spent the whole night being woken up by her tiptoeing backwards and forwards to the loo and making a big noise about not waking us up.

'GO BACK TO SLEEP! IT'S JUST ME GOING TO THE LOO. OW! WHO PUT THAT TABLE THERE? YOU MADE ME STUB MY TOE. (Silence) AND WHERE'S THE LIGHT SWITCH? WHO KNOWS WHERE THE LIGHT SWITCH IS? SOMEBODY MUST KNOW WHERE ... IT'S OK, I'VE FOUND IT!' The light was on and off all

night – every time she went in, and every time she came out. And every time she came out we got a blow by blow commentary. 'Nothing this time. Expect it's too early. I'll try again in ten minutes.' Ten minutes later she went in again, only this time she fell asleep on the pan and her snoring kept us awake.

2.21 a.m. – 'If Granny's bagsed the loo all the time,' I said to Mum, 'what do we do if we need to go?'

'We we?' giggled Will, who can sometimes be pathetic.

'You go Au Naturel,' mumbled Mum.

'Au what?' I said.

'Naturel,' said Mum 'I'll tell you about it in the morning.'

I thought Naturel was a yoghurt. So I peed in a yoghurt pot, resealed the lid and popped it back in the fridge. After that I was able to concentrate better on schemes to get me back for filming.

2.47 a.m. - Tried the old stomachache scam to get Mum and Dad to take me home. I groaned that I'd got food poisoning from the greasy chef's spit. Mum was less than sympathetic.

'If you're sick one more time, Alistair, I shall take you to the nearest hospital and dump you on the doorstep!' She would and all. She's *that* neglectful—

HANG ON A SQUIDDLY! DAD DOESN'T WEAR A HEARING AID! UGH! THAT IS SO SICK!

3.12 a.m. - Mr E has just joined in caravan smell-fest with a rootin' tootin' symphony of peeps and parps. Why do little dogs' farts always smell like dead woodland creatures? Someone had to take dog for a walk.

'Can't we just open the door and let him run wild?' I suggested. Apparently not. We were in a dangerous lorry park.

DANGEROUS /deindzeres/ adj. – Involving or causing danger. Such as little boys wandering around lorry parks in the dark when lorry drivers can't see them and are likely to reverse over them without ever knowing they're there. Apart from noticing a little bump when they run over boy's neck.

So Dad volunteered me on account of him having done all the driving all day – like I really could have driven if I'd wanted!

ME: Dad, I know I'm only eleven and it's still six years till I can take my test, but could I drive for a bit?

DAD: Why, sure, son. Just remember to put your foot down through this built-up area and don't stop for traffic lights. Gee, Ma, ain't it grand seeing our little nipper behind the wheel at last!

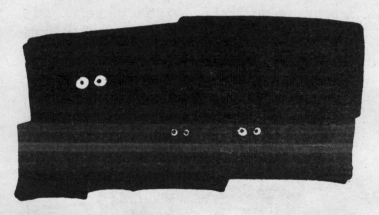

So there I was in my pyjamas and wellingtons walking an ugly pug and a bubble-wrapped cat through a lorry park at three in the morning waiting for them to pee and poo! Was this really what I was put on earth to do? Suddenly had brilliant idea based on that film called *The Incredible Journey* in which three scabby pets walk all the way home and sleep in barns. If I could hide Mr E and Napoleon, then say that they had escaped and were last seen heading back home, then we would HAVE to go home too. To look after them. It's a well-known fact that pets can't look after themselves unless they have got either:

1. a can opener, or
2. a steady supply of wild garden animals willing to commit suicide so that the pet can eat.

3.24 a.m. – Hid cat and dog in boot of car with strips of cold, grey bacon from café dustbin and hubcap full of water. Then ran back into caravan waving leads and shouting, 'They've gone. They've gone. They've slipped their leads and gone home!'

Everyone was supposed to help look for them, but Will hates waking up to hunt for pets, apparently, Mel was writing another LUVTXT to RDNY, because her mobile was suddenly working again, and Granny didn't want to stray too far from the loo. So it was just me, Mum and Dad.

3.39 a.m. – Dad said, 'Do you really think

135

they're clever enough to find their way home?'

'No,' said Mum. 'They'll be hiding round here somewhere.'

I needed a new idea. 'I've just remembered,' I said. 'I think I saw a stalker in the car park earlier . . .

PAY ATTENTION, ALL YOU POTENTIAL REVENGERS!

This is a classic example of how painstaking preparation pays off in the field. Preparation = 112% worth it!

. . . Maybe he's snatched the animals just to get at you, Mum. Maybe he's holding them hostage AT HOME and he's going to ask a price. Yes, that's it!'

'No. If he's going to kidnap them the last place he'll take them is home,' said Mum. 'We should stay here.'

I panicked. 'Well if they're not at home we've got to be at home for the phone call demanding the ransom,' I said. 'Poor little things. They must be so scared. How much would you give to get them back?'

'Everything,' said Mum.

That includes little me, of course!

'Your house? Your car?' I asked.
'Everything,' she said. 'I love them.'
'All your money?'
'Everything!'
'*Towed in the Hole!*?'
Silence. Long pause.
'Well maybe not my career,' said Mum, 'but everything else.'

Then Dad heard barking and saw long trail of bubble wrap leading to boot. Game over! I tried to explain how they had got into boot, but nobody believed my story that they had both been shrunk by an alien space ray to the size of a mouse and had crawled up the exhaust pipe to escape from being beamed up, and then the ray had worn off and they'd grown back again. Instead, everyone went back to bed, leaving me to clean up the mess in the boot.

Made up this poem while mopping:

Just wait Toopac Nijinski,
And do not give up hope,
I'll act you in the film
If I have to kill the Pope!

6.08 a.m. – Slept briefly between 6.00 and 6.07. Managed very short Spanish dream in which I parked caravan in bull-ring then joined crowd and waited for my family to open door in morning and step out into path of angry bull!

Everyone in foul mood as nobody got any sleep. Who needs a luxury holiday in sunny Spain when a weekend caravanning in the car park of the Grease and Bucket Service Station can be had at a fraction of the cost?!!!!!

Granny got up early to be first in the loo. Not the pretty dawn chorus I was expecting to hear – the strangled strains of the Lesser Scrabbled Granny Bird. Mum took the three of us outside to demonstrate the Au Naturel method of looing-it. It involved a spade, a hole and a rolled-up newspaper. I have always thought the one thing that distinguished the human race from the lowly beasts was our mastery of hygienic toilet facilities. I was wrong. We are clearly no higher up the evolutionary ladder than bears.

Finding privacy was hard in a car park. There were interested truckers waking up in every cab. It was so embarrassing we couldn't go.

'Don't be so vain,' said Mum. 'Nobody's interested in you.'

'Yes they are!' I said, trying to make myself as thin as a lamppost so that I couldn't be seen behind it. Mel was waving

Do not mean this obviously. Hence use of five exclamation marks, which means it's a joke.

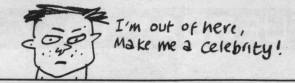

I'm out of here,
Make me a celebrity!

at the truckers, who didn't need much encouragement to riot. It was safer in the caravan.

On way back in, discovered that the car CD/radio had been nicked through open window. It was of course MY fault for being sick so that the window had to be left open overnight. Now that he was deprived of music, Will hated me more than ever. He hated me, robbers, car parks, truckers, spit chicken and robbers again. He wanted to seal the robbers' heads inside a huge stadium speaker then

A mashed Swede!

play Death Metal at supersonic levels till their earholes bled and their brains turned to mashed swede. But he couldn't do that, so he pushed me into some stinging nettles instead. I am now covered in white blobs and look like a plucked chicken.

To add insult to injury, Mum and Dad have promised big brother that they will

make another detour after mobile phone shop to buy new CD/radio for his music. Do I have INVISIBLE stamped on my forehead? When I speak are my words carried off on the backs of little fairies so that they do not reach my parents' ears? Then why does everybody jump to attention for Will and Mel and NEVER for me?

COMPARE & CONTRAST

ALISTAIR (*most reasonable tones*): Can I stay at home to make a film that will turn me into a happy, well-balanced and rich celebrity, Mummy?

MUMMY: Who's seen my mobile phone? Oh, for goodness' sake, Alistair, stop being such a waste of space and find it!

Now compare and contrast . . .

WILLIAM or MEL (*full of unattractive attitude*): Oi, slag! I want this and that. Get it. All right?

MUMMY: Of course, darling. I'll just stop what I'm doing and cater to your every whim.

See what I mean?

In caravan Granny was tucking into usual healthy breakfast of yoghurt. She wasn't sure about new lemony flavour – bit sour for her liking. Can't think why . . .

Today we are visiting Mr Bloodworthe, maker of fine, traditional Somerset black puddings. That's made with blood, that is. PUKE! Mr Bloodworthe doesn't sound like he comes from Somerset. My guess is Transylvania. Bought anti-vampire garlic in town just in case, while Dad bought Mel new phone and Will new CD player for car. Will wanted one with woofers and tweeters and a subsonic range that only dolphins can hear, but the electronic guts would have taken up too much space in the boot. Will suggested we put the electronic guts in the caravan, but Dad said the caravan was for living in, not for towing Will's CD player. Well done, Dad ... for once! I think he is getting fed up at all the money he's spending!

Mel had strop again on pavement outside phone shop. New phone didn't get signal

either. Did I not tell her that it was the signal not the phone? If she'd listen to her little brother occasionally she might learn something. I offered to see if I could mend it for her. All I did really was change the ring tone from one that she loved to one that she hated – *Mr Moustache* by Nirvana. It's really really funny and will really annoy her every time it rings!

Asked Mum and Dad, *politely*, if I might have a little present too, but was told 'no'. I was the cause of all our family's problems, and had to behave before I got a gift. Right! While everyone else finished shopping I went back to car and took action!

Wrote note on bit of scrap paper and put it under the windscreen wiper. I made each letter a different size to make it look like I was mad.

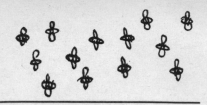

Then I lined up the Sting for Mel. I made a wasp trap by opening the miniature jar of honey and leaving it on car bonnet. There was nothing miniature about the wasps I trapped! I made them angry by calling them rude names, like 'You w***** wasp!' then placed jar on back ledge of car and covered it with my baseball cap so that my beautiful stingers couldn't escape! Wasp bomb primed and ready to Aaaaaaaaaagggggghhhh!

When the family got back I was sitting innocently on the back seat of the car, knowing that Will and Mel would want me out and in the caravan. Dad had bought a mystery present for Granny. What she wants with a Tupperware sugar bowl is anybody's guess. And in a rush of blood to the head he bought a nail file for himself, which he's hidden in his socks in case he needs to break out of prison!

True to form, Mel and Will ordered me out of the car and into the caravan.

I pretended to be upset, but wasn't

Big brothers and sisters are more predictable than thick sheep.

145

really. Just took my cap and went, stopping only to say this to Mum:

'Oh Mummy, have you seen that funny note on your windscreen? It was left by a man who I thought was a traffic warden, but up close he had too many hairs in his ears – he was a real mean looking son of a gun, a scary, heartless, cold-blooded whisky-drinking no-good bum.'

'Language, Alistair.'

'Sorry, Granny.'

THE GREAT GROSS UNFAIRNESSES OF LiFE
No. 64 – The Lippy Granny

How come Granny can swear like a footballer and write rude words in Scrabble

and nobody ever tells her off? It's like she's in charge of her own little universe, and everyone who comes within half a mile of her body has to obey the rules of her little universe, whether they've got their own little universe with *its* own rules or not! So why are the rules for Granny's little universe better than the rules for my little universe? It is so unfair it makes me want to swear.

But I'm not allowed to, so I won't. Which is exactly my point, as it happens.

Mum said if the stalker was that scary maybe she should do what the note said and go home. I screamed 'Yes!' a bit too loudly.

'Although,' she went on, 'if he doesn't

know where I live he can't be a very good stalker. And his spelling's atrocious, which leads me to believe that he can't read, so he won't be able to find us on a map. No, I think I'll just give the note to the police and let their forensic chaps search it for clues. They're bound to find out who wrote it. And when they do, they'll bang him up in rusty leg irons for at least twenty years. By which time any career prospects that he might have had – in the theatre or films, for example – would have withered on the vine due to ugly old age, rickety bones and hair loss.'

'Is that what happens to stalkers?' I asked.

'If they're lucky,' she said.

I felt sick again. Luckily Dad wouldn't have the police involved in case they recognized him as the Tooting Jury Jumper. He begged Mum to let him go home, but she wanted blood! Puddings, to be precise.

In the caravan, Mr E climbed the walls to get away from me and Napoleon flung himself at the closed window like a frog in a blender. After incident in boot of car I think they thought I was a torturer. I

would never knowingly hurt a dumb animal. Unless it was my big brother or sister of course.

Granny caught Napoleon by the back leg and wired the Tupperware sugar bowl onto his head.

'It's a little catty crash helmet,' she said. 'To stop him from hurting himself during a mad spell.' She got it on just in time. The next thing we knew the wasp bomb had exploded!

The caravan skidded to the left as Dad pulled over. Napoleon flew across the sofa and would have brained himself on the floor if it hadn't been for the Tupperware sugar bowl. Mr E was not so lucky. He ended up sitting on a tap like a glove puppet with a look of wide-eyed surprise on his face.

Outside, it was brilliant. Mel had stripped off her jumper and was dancing a screaming jig by the side of the road. The wasp had gone down her neck then come out again. Dad used her jumper to flick it out of the sky then crush it to death on the tarmac. This brought more tears from Mel on account of the jumper having cost her £35 and Dad having just squashed insect juice into it! He'll have to buy her

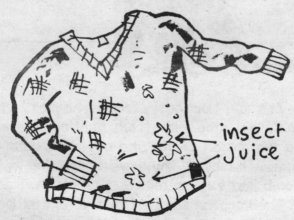

insect juice

another one now! Soon he will flip at spending all this wasted money and when he does he'll *insist* we go home. And Mum

I wasn't in her vest, obviously - she was. ←

will be too scared of his manliness to say no. Ho-ho! Was there no end to my genius?

I was really hoping that Mel would blow up with an allergic reaction to wasp stings so that we'd have to go home immediately, but the only reaction she had was to march up to me in her vest and bash me round the ears.

I played the innocent. 'What's going on here?' I cried. 'Mummy she's attacking me for no reason. Blame the wasp, Mel, not me!' But I think I may have been laughing – I know I snorted accidentally and a stream of snot squirted out of my nose – because nobody came to my rescue.

SUPERSONIC SNOT STREAM

I was sat on the back seat between Will and Mel where Mum could see me. We were told to play nice games until we got to Mr Bloodworthe's. We played I Spy, but everything that Mel and Will spied hurt me. They spied a Fist that hit me; a Pinch that made me shriek; an Ear Twist that tweaked my ear. I complained that they

were cheating, because two-word objects weren't allowed. So the next word was Dead Leg, which Mel said really fast like it was one word, which everyone knows it ISN'T! It still hurt, though, and my leg was still dead.

Then we played Botticelli, which is a stupid game where you have to think of a person who's dead or alive, and the others get twenty questions to find out who you are. Mel and Will were really amusing. They made me choose and then said, 'You're dead.'

'No I'm not,' I replied.

'You are,' they said.

'Who's answering the questions?' I shouted. 'I'm the one who knows who I've chosen.'

'And you're dead,' grinned Will.

'I'm Kylie Minogue!' I protested.

'You're still dead,' whispered Mel, 'when we get you home!'

After that Will and Mel didn't want to

Although that might have had something to do with the number of sweets I'd eaten.

play with me again. I suggested Number Plates, and Counting Sheep and Cows, and Bridges, but no one was up for it.

'Come on,' I said. 'Someone else choose something!'

'I hate little brothers,' said Will.

'We'll play that then,' I said.

'It's not a game,' he said, 'it's true.'

This was turning out to be the longest car journey of my life. Admittedly it had quite a lot to do with Dad driving at the speed of snail and Mum calling out the wrong directions all the time, but it was so boring that my teeth grew fur.

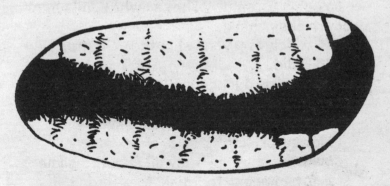

Then Mel's phone rang.

'Isn't that *Mr Moustache* by Nirvana?' I asked. That earned me a slapped head.

She answered the phone in an angry

whisper: 'I thought I told you never to call me when I'm in the car with my family! Texts only!' Then she went quiet and her face changed colour from pink to white. Then she stared at the phone and pressed END. 'He hung up,' she said.

'Who did?' asked Mum.

'An American,' said Mel. 'He said, "Melanie Fury? We think you stink too." And then he rang off.'

'Maybe you've got a stalker too,' I said, wondering why he was an American. 'We should definitely go home now, Mum.'

'It was a wrong number,' said Mum.

'Yeah!' I said. 'That's what all her boyfriends think!'

To which everyone shouted, 'Shut up!'

So I did.

There was a long long long silence. Then Mel said, 'Do I stink?'

'I can't smell anything,' said Will.

'Not surprising,' I said.

'Will you shut up!' they all shouted again. I was beginning to think they didn't like me.

I *knew* they didn't like me ten seconds later when the second wasp crawled out of Dad's seat and stuck his stinger into my

154

arm. It was so painful that I saw angels and heard choirs singing. I was sobbing and wailing like a big girl.

'I want to go home!' I cried.

But Mum said it was just a little sting and we should press on. 'We're hours late as it is,' she said. 'Mr Bloodworthe's black puddings won't keep for ever.'

'Why not?' asked Dad.

'Because he only uses the freshest blood,' said Mum 'or the puddings clot.'

We were six hours late when we arrived at Black Pudding Farm. Farmer Bloodworthe was furious. He'd been up all night preparing the black puddings for Mum and now they were ruined. He didn't want nothing to do with Mum's stupid TV programme. He pushed her away. Dad muscled in, asking him if he wanted some, whereupon the farmer said, 'Yes please,' and struck Dad on the nose. That was the turning point. After that, the farmer became all friendly and apologetic. Mainly, I suspect, because Dad's nose had started to bleed.

'Don't waste it!' he yelled, holding up a flowerpot to catch the drips. 'I can use that. Come inside!'

It had started to rain again, so we waited in the caravan with Granny while she built more travel armour for Napoleon. He was still wrapped in bubble wrap and still wearing the Tupperware sugar bowl, but now she had hung him off the floor in a pair of old tights that she'd tied round the light bulb. She'd cut catty paw holes in the tights so that he could stick his paws out. The idea was quite good actually. He swung with the movement of the caravan and didn't hit anything. As I said several times, it was Purrfect Protection, but Will and Mel wouldn't laugh even though I could tell they were dying to.

Granny was in the loo humming hits from *Abba – The Looky-Likies* and keeping us abreast of her progress. 'Still no luck!' she called out cheerily.

'We'll have a little celebration when you manage something,' I said, trying to make a friend out of one of my family.

7.55 p.m. – Five minutes to go till webcam meeting with Revengers. I need fresh ideas. The Revengers are my only hope if I

am to fulfil my destiny and become a beautiful shining star in that great big sky known as Celebrity-bigsky. Five minutes to go and all will be well. The clock is ticking.

7.58 p.m. – Mel just had another fit. Her phone has stopped working again.

'It's because we're in the back of beyond,' I told her. Then I added

dramatically, 'A forgotten spot where the devil rules!' I could see from her face that she was scared. It suddenly occurred to me that if I could get her to scream and burst a blood vessel maybe *she* could persuade Mum to take us home. 'Am I the only one to think this farmer's up to no good?' I said, pressing further into Horror territory. 'Do the words cold-blooded murderer remind you of anyone?'

'I'm borrowing Mum's,' she said suddenly, storming out to the car, where Mum had hidden her mobile.

'No!' I screamed. 'That's not fair. I was using that!' I tried to stop her going, but she slammed the caravan door in my face. Then I heard something I hadn't heard in ages, and it wasn't the low throaty grunt of an albino badger. It was Will.

Shutting a caravan door in my face... geddit?!.'

'I hate murderers,' he moaned. 'I hate farmers. I hate blood pudding. I'd run away from here right now if I knew where I was . . . or didn't hate running.'

9.12 p.m. – I have waited for over an hour for that Love-Nazi of a big sister to finish her phone call. Mum and Dad will be back soon and then I won't be able to speak to the Revengers. Have no choice but to abandon webcam and phone instead. It's quicker. That is assuming Mel ever stops TxtMsging Rdny.

9.22 p.m.- Hallelujah! She has finished! Snatched phone off Mel and dialled Ralph's house. Luckily Aaron was with him. I told them how every one of our brilliant plans had failed and how we were camping on a murderer's farm in Somerset.

Ralph yelped with an idea. 'Keep saying that the farmer is a murderer,' he said, 'then add that he is putting human beings into his black puddings like Sweeney Todd. Find an axe and spade and bury your arm in the soil, then pretend that your hand belongs to a dead body!'

'I couldn't touch a dead hand,' I said. 'Or dead fingers. Or anything dead really.'

'I could touch a dead nose,' said Aaron, 'because a nose can be quite cold anyway.'

I touched my nose. 'You're right,' I said.

'Look,' sighed Ralph. 'It's not a dead hand, it's your hand pretending to be dead.'

'I think this might be a bit too complicated,' I said.

'Just trust me,' said Ralph. 'It'll work.'

'But what if it doesn't?'

'If it doesn't, put some body parts in a couple of pies and accidentally find them.'

'Like a leg you mean?'

'I wouldn't have thought a leg would fit in a pie,' said Aaron. 'Unless it was a long tall pie in the shape of a leg.'

LEG PIE

'Then don't put a leg in,' shouted Ralph. 'Put in something smaller.'

'Like a midget's leg?' I said.

'WILL YOU FORGET LEGS!' screamed Ralph. 'Put in something like a toe or an ear.'

'Where am I going to find something like that?' I said.

'Well, if he's a murderer like you say he is,' said Aaron, 'there are bound to be dozens of them lying around the farm. Unless the pigs have eaten them, of course. Pigs have a nose for a nose.'

Just then I lost sound. The phone battery was on its way out, so I called it a day. Couldn't resist sneaking a look at Mel's TXTMSGS to RDNY though. They were every bit as sloshy as I knew they would be. She had written:

ULITEMYFIRE, RDNY

And he had replied:

GOOD

Then she had written:

I LUV U DAY BY DAY
& YEAR BY YEAR
MORE & MORE
TEAR BY TEAR

And he had written back:

WOTSWEATHERLIKE?

And she had finished with:

TAKEMYHANDTAKEMY-
HOLELIFE2
COSICANTSOS
FALLINGINLUVWIVU

To which he had signed off with:

WOTEVR

I thought RDNY needed one final TXT from Mel to let him know where he stood.

URBIGGSTB*T*D
INHOLEWORLD
LUVMEL

That'll teach her!

Then put mobile on charge and returned to glove compartment, wiping off my fingerprints so Mum would find TXTMSGS and think culprit was Mel! Has she got it coming!

Found ear in cupboard in caravan. It was Mr E's. Not Mr E's ear. It was a pig's ear

I've been wondering where it went

for Mr E to eat. Sometimes animals can be such . . . animals! I mean, I could never eat a part of another animal's body. Apart from chops and steaks and bacon butties, obviously. And fish fingers. Then I took the Au Naturel trowel from under the sink and went outside, *apparently* to do my business like a bear. Before I went, I upped the spookiness of the farm by saying, 'Wish me luck. This may be the last time you see me alive, Melanie and William. Next time you set eyes on me could be on the cold meat counter at Tesco!'

They did not seemed bothered.

Outside, I found an axe in a log shed and threw it into some nearby bushes, where it could be found as the murder weapon. Then, behind the caravan, I dug a hole with the trowel and buried my arm, leaving my hand and fingers poking out through the soil. Then I shouted my lungs off.

Mr E got to me first, sniffed my fingers and cocked his leg on them. It was all warm. I couldn't push him away because I was pretending that the wet fingers were

the lifeless fingers of a dead body and the reason I had my arm in the ground was because I was trying to pull the dead arm out.

Mel, Will and Granny arrived to see what the noise was about.

'Murder!' I shuddered. 'Murder! We've got to get out of here now and GO HOME. Look ye, here is proof that there is bad stuff a-goin' on at Blood Pudding Farm. Forsooth, a severed arm!'

girly squeal →

MEGA DEATH METAL 04

Mel screamed as I knew she would. 'Yes!' she wailed. 'We must go home.'

'We must,' I cried. 'Or you'll be next in the pudding, Mel. And once you've been baked in a pudding, that's it! There's no text messaging in Hell!'

William was trying hard to stay cool and not be freaked by the dead flesh, but when Mr E brushed against his leg he screamed like a girl spotting a mouse. That set off

the stupid dog, who attacked the dead
hand and tried to gnaw the fingers to the
bone. I couldn't show pain so I beat the
ugly pug with my free hand and shouted,
'Get him off the evidence!'

Granny flew into a rage. 'I am disgusted
at you, Alistair,' she said. 'First your dirty
swearing tongue and now you're beating up
poor defenceless creatures! It'll be prison
soon for you, my lad!'

Then suddenly Mum and Dad were there
wanting to know what all the fuss was
about and Farmer Bloodworthe had found
the axe in the bush and was running
towards me with it raised above his head.

167

I thought he was going to chop my arm off and did what I should not have done. I whipped my arm out of the ground!

Everyone stared at my muddy arm and then at me. I sensed a feeling not unlike anger.

'Oh look,' I said, shaking my hand like it was the first time I'd ever seen it. 'It was *my* arm all along. What a chump I am! I didn't know it was *my* arm, because the other arm *was* there. The chopped off murdered one. It was! I promise! Oh come on, guys! Why does nobody ever believe me? That is so unfair! Wait! I've got it. I know what happened.' They couldn't wait to hear my excuse. 'The buried arm must have scuttled away when I put *my* arm into the earth to grab it. Yes! That's it! It wasn't dead at all. It was the arm of an Egyptian zombie, which could live on detached from its body! Yes, of course. Simple, really, when you think about it.' The lie wasn't

working. 'Actually I think I saw a puma steal it. Can we go home now, Mummy? I'm hungry.'

We could not go home. Even though Dad thought the arm was real and was sitting in the car with the engine running, we stayed the night in one of the farmer's fields. Will and Mel said I'd gone mad and because of that wouldn't sleep in the same caravan as me. So Mum put me in the tent and Dad had to help me put it up. We struggled. Every time we stood the centre pole upright, sections dropped off the bottom. We gave up after an hour, when the tent was still only two feet tall, which meant that when Dad finally plucked up the courage to ask me for a chat, we were lying down next to each other like two pencils in a box. Dad made me promise that I wouldn't phone the police about tonight's murder.

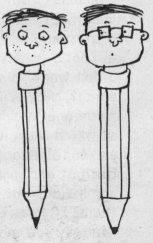

'I promise,' I said. 'But you do know that was *my* hand in the ground, don't you? And I made up all that stuff about a murderer's arm.'

Dad looked confused. He is not the full ticket.

Over a late supper, he fell for the pig's ear in the black pudding too. At first I asked if anyone else had found tufts of hair in their supper. That stopped everyone eating, especially when I showed them a chewed tuft and asked what type of hair they thought it might be.

'Is it a moustache, do you think, Mel?'

Then I produced the ear and pretended to faint. 'Oh, to think I nearly ate it!' I whispered dramatically. 'A *human* ear.' Mum laughed and told me not to be so ridiculous. 'But this is proof that there's man meat inside these blood puddings,' I protested.

That's when Dad said he definitely didn't want to stay now, and because *he'd* said it, Mel, Will and Granny all said it too. 'Four-one! We're going home!' I announced, at which Mum went off on one.

'You all want nice holidays, and new clothes, and mobile phones and car radios,' she yelled, 'but who do you think pays for them? If I don't get *Towed in the Hole!* onto the telly you can kiss goodbye to the lot.'

170

Mel screamed. Mr E was chewing the pig's ear and had dropped a white, blood-less lump of bristle and gristle onto her foot.

'If you keep screaming like that, Melanie,' Mum growled, 'we *will* go home!'

STOP THE WORLD! NOW THIS WAS PROGRESS!

This was the best news I'd had in days. Making Mel scream was as easy as shout-ing, 'Look out! There's a wasp on your leg!'

She screamed again.

'I'm warning you,' said Mum.

'And I'm going to the toilet,' said Granny. 'You're all as bad as each other.'

'Shut up!' said Will. 'I hate arguments.'

'Well I'm not going to the loo Au Naturel,' I said. 'Not with a murderer on the loose.'

'There's nothing out there,' said Mum.

'There was an arm,' said Dad.

'Yeah, imagine it, Mel,' I said. 'There you are squatting on a grassy knoll when a severed arm bursts out of its stinking grave and grabs your bum!' She screamed again. 'She screamed again, Mum, *twice*. Can we go home now?'

I think Mum and I had reached another Mason and Pearson hairbrush moment – spiky side down! Luckily Mel's mobile rang and saved me from a brushing.

It was a TXTMSG from RDNY.

THEREISNOMORE2SAY.
IFUFEELLIKETHATITISOVR
NEVRTXTMEAGEN
RDNY

'But I only told him I loved him!' wailed Mel. She ran into the caravan and slammed the door.

I think that might have been a reply to the MSG I sent! Ho-ho!

172

3.00 a.m. – Alone in tent. Bored. Called Mel's mobile for fun and sang along with *Mr Moustache*. Watched as caravan window was opened and mobile phone thrown out. It squelched to silence in mud.

3.15 a.m. – Feel like dam is about to burst. Mel is broken. Will is scared. Dad is loop the loop, and Mum is starting to crack. Tomorrow morning I, Alistair Van de Fury, will take my little Dutch finger out of the hole! I have a plan . . .

When everyone got up I was gone. Left note on sleeping bag to get them dead worried.

DEAR FAMILY,
SNATCHED BY FOX AS I SLEPPT HENCE SLIGHTLY RUSHED NOTE AND BAD SPELLINK. WAS MILES AWAY BY TIME I WOKE UP. WILL MAKE MY OWN WAHAY HOME WHEN I CAN ESCAPE. DON'T WURRY. IT'S A VERY NICE FOX WITH COOL LAYER, INKLUDIN COLOUR TV, DVD AND X-BOX. SO PLENNY LUVELY STUFF TO DO. YOU GO ON AND HAVE A NICE HOLIDAY. I'LL CATCH YOU BACK AT HOME IN A FORTNIGHT.

WISHING I WAS STILL WITH YOU, BUT I'M NOT. TCH! THAT'S LIFE, I SUPPOSE.

YUR EVER LUVING SON/BROTHER/GRANDSON

ALISTAIR (FURY)

I was actually lying in the bushes about one hundred metres from the caravan, so I watched them all searching for me. I had hoped that they would just pack up and go on without me, thinking that I was safe with the nice fox with the kicking entertainment system, but they kept on searching. Hour after hour. It is so typical of my family that the one time I DON'T want them to care about me they DO!

Eventually they got so close to my hide-out that discovery was inevitable. Had to unleash Plan B. Filled my mouth with toothpaste and mixed it up with spit until there was white foam running down my chin.

This was how they found me.

'I think I need to see my doctor,' I frothed. 'My favourite one. The one at home. Sadly, as you know, I was kidnapped by a fox last night and I think he's given me rabies!'

Everyone panicked. Well, Mum ran back to the caravan and fetched a glass of water.

'Quick!' she said. 'Drink that.' So I did, thinking she was going to take me home straight afterwards. 'That should rinse the toothpaste out your mouth!' she said.

I was flabbergasted. 'How did you know it was toothpaste?' I said.

'Because if you have rabies you also have a fear of water,' she said briskly. What a CHEAP CHEESY CHEAT! 'And now that we've found you we can head off to our next kitchen of call. Cornwall!'

Cornwall! CORNWALL! That's like, 'Next stop the South Pole!' It's miles away. You need dog packs and food rations to get down to Cornwall. Satellite tracking systems are recommended! I'm meant to be on set, filming my way to super celebrity status in four days' time

and Mum wants to take us on a six-month overland trek to Cornwall!

Face it, Alistair Fury, you are never going to get off this holiday. You are never going to be a film star. You are never going to be honoured by the Academy with an Oscar for Best Actor Ever in a Film Made in Tooting with Singing and Dancing unless a miracle happens!

I was numb to Mel's threats of mutilations for muddying her mobile.

'If I were you, I'd watch my bum,' she said.

'Watch your bum?' I said. 'I can't watch anything else, Mel. It's so big it should be in a circus. And I think you mean "back".'

'I know what I mean,' she said.

Then we were off. I wanted to go in the caravan, but Mel made me sit on a cushion on the back seat of the car.

'It's because you're so little,' she told me. 'It'll help you see out of the windscreen.'

I didn't want to see out of the windscreen. I didn't want a cushion. But Mel insisted.

'But I don't want to,' I said.

'But I insist.'

'But I don't want to.'

'But I insist.'

'But I don't w—'

'Just sit on the flipping cushion!' screamed Mum.

I sat on the cushion.

An hour later we were lost, driving around in circles again, when the cushion took on a life of its own. For a second I thought I had wet myself, what with the activity in my pants and the warm spreading feeling down my thighs. Then something bit me. I leaped up off the cushion and screamed to blue blazes.

'What's the matter?' smirked Mel. 'Ants in your pants?' Which is what it was, of course. Warrior Biting Ants! 'Oh, sorry, Alice, I must have left the cushion on an ants' nest before I put it in the car!!!'

There was so much pain in my manly lower half that I had to take my trousers off again. Unfortunately, as Mel and Will wouldn't budge up, I had to lean forward to undo my flies. In so doing, I leaned on Dad's neck and pushed his head down onto his chest. Suddenly he couldn't see out front and the car and the caravan mounted the West Camel roundabout, squashed all the flowers, shot down the other side, crashed through a hedge, jack-knifed across a dirt track and came to rest wedged against a shiny steel fence with barbed wire on top.

In the silence that followed William started to cry. At least I thought it was crying. It was laughter. It was like he'd just woken out of a deep sleep.

'That was brilliant,' he whooped. 'That was better than anything at Thorpe Park. And look at that wicked sign on the fence!'

DANGER! UNAUTHORIZED ENTRY MAY RESULT IN SERIOUS LOSS OF LIFE!

There was an American flag underneath and the words **US DEFENCE BASE.**

Above our heads a video camera whirred. It swung round and pointed at the car. Next to the camera was a loudspeaker, which suddenly coughed into life.

I noticed and shall never forget. In fact my skin's still tingling with a desire to pay her back. Or is that the poison from the ant bites?

'Stop, sir! You are in breach of the law,' said a computerized American voice. 'Lay down your weapons and step out of the car with your hands above your head. This is an Automated Self-Arresting VideoCop and this message will replay in five seconds' time. *Beep. Beep. Beep. Beep.* Stop, sir! You are in breach of the law. Lay down your weapons and step out of the car with your hands above your head. This is an Automated Self-Arresting VideoCop and this message will replay in five seconds time. *Beep . . .'*

Then we heard a distant police siren.

Dad panicked. 'I'm going to prison,' he cried.

Mum didn't seem all that bothered. 'I hope so,' she said crossly. 'I've never seen such bad driving.' I think she was angry because her work on *Towed in the Hole!* had been rather permanently messed up.

Mel had gone quiet and was trying not to be noticed in case someone pointed out that she had caused the crash with her ants.

Meanwhile, I had got out of the car and

removed my trousers to scatter the biters and Will couldn't wait to meet Robocop.

It was Dad who was flapping. He hauled me back into the car and, with doors still open, restarted the engine and accelerated hard. The wheels skidded in the grass, then gripped and shot us away from the fence, pulling the caravan into line behind us. Then we bumped off down the track, swung left through another hedge, rejoined a different road to the one we'd crashed off, and sped off as fast as we could.

'Where are we going?' asked Mum. 'I have crabs waiting for me in Cornwall.'

'Tonight we lie low,' said Dad. 'Tomorrow, when the heat is off, we'll head for St

Ives.' He'd been watching too many gangster movies.

We drove for about half an hour, then pulled into a field and hid up behind a tall hedge. It was only then that Mum remembered Granny. The inside of the caravan was upside down. The floor was covered in cushions and pans. Cupboards and drawers had spilled out over the floor. Mr E was skewered on top of that same painful tap, with that same look of surprise. And Napoleon had bounced off the walls and wedged under the grill. Luckily Granny had packed him into a polystyrene bun, made from the packaging from Mel's new mobile and Will's CD/radio. He wasn't hurt, but he looked like an uncooked cat burger. Granny was nowhere to be seen.

'I'm in the loo,' she called out. 'All that excitement and terror, I thought it might make me go.' It hadn't.

Dad, Will and I made camp. We broke branches off trees to camouflage the vehicles.

'In case the police attack us from the air,' explained Dad. He called the camp Fortress Fury, which Will thought was excellent. In fact, since his family had become outlaws, Will suddenly thought *everything* was excellent. He even thanked me for handing him a piece of bracken. I hadn't seen him this happy for months.

Meanwhile, moaners Mum and Mel moped about in the caravan while Granny played Scrabble on her own. Mum was depressed because Michael hadn't phoned with news from the BBC, and Mel was depressed because she really really loved RDNY apparently, and now she was on the shelf at sixteen. Serves her right. I hope

184

she dies an old maid and is eaten alive by ants.

Then we heard music from the field beyond the one we were in and William punched the air.

'This just gets better and better!' he cried. He grabbed Mel and they ran towards the noise.

'Where are you going?' screamed Mum.

'To get a new boyfriend,' shouted Mel.

'Can I come?' I yelled. Then added quickly. 'Not to get a new boyfriend, obviously. I'm not a girl.'

'No!' said Mel. 'You're way too little!'

It was an outdoor concert. Like a festival thing. They'd heard the bands warming up. As night fell, the music

started proper and the air rocked. I sat outside staring at the sky, listening to the sounds and thinking about what might have been. I'd never make it home in time for filming now. Probably never make it home ever, what with Dad being a real-life fugitive. Gone was my fifteen minutes of fame, my chance to dance in the sunshine and act at the feet of the gods. From now on I was just plain Alistair Who? – ordinary bloke, nobody special, poor and unfamous like everyone else in the world.

Goodbye, Hollywood. Hello, Day-Glo holes in the road.

FURYWOOD

ABOUT TO BURST

A hand tapped me on the shoulder. I must have drifted off. It was a bloke wearing muddy clothes, a black bin liner and long hair. He had a sort of straggly beard too, which if I'm honest, and without being rude, would have looked better on a goat.

YOU DECIDE

'We were told there was a toilet up here,' he said.

'We?' I said. The man pointed to a long line of people that stretched back across the field towards the music.

'Can we, like, use it? The toilets are mashed down there.'

I don't know whether it was the sight of 500 hippies queuing up for our caravan loo; or the fact that one of the people in the queue said to Mum, 'I know you. Didn't you used to be famous?' or the sound of

Granny in distress when she realized that she would not be able to go to the loo for three days unless she joined the back of the queue, but something flipped a switch in Mum's head.

BEFORE

AFTER

She marched up to the camouflage and pulled a branch off the car.

'What are you doing?' panicked Dad.

'We're going home,' she announced.

I was, like . . .

WHAT?

'Come on. Pack up. We're going home.'

After all my efforts, all that blood, sweat

and lies, why had she suddenly decided that *now* was the time to go home? 'Michael hasn't phoned me. That can only mean he hasn't persuaded the BBC to take my programme. It's a waste of time going on. *Towed in the Hole!* is finished. Besides, I hate caravanning and I don't like sharing my loo with a tribe of Neanderthals.' That was what she called the hippies.

I was ecstatic. I was back on track to be a celebrity! Dad was jumping for joy. Now he could go home and hide in the attic. Granny was smiling too. She hated watching Pet Pinball and her dicky bowels meant that she wasn't seeing as much of the countryside as she'd have liked. I threw myself at Mum and gave her a huge kiss and told her that there wasn't another mum in the whole world that I loved quite as much. She said she was glad to hear it.

Then after the joy, the agony! We couldn't go home, because selfish pleasure-seekers Mel and Will, who never think of anyone but themselves, weren't there!

'Don't worry,' I said. 'They hate this holiday as much as the rest of us. They're desperate to get home too. They'll be here soon. And then we can go!'

We scared off the hippies by throwing bars of soap at them, packed up the caravan and waited.

And waited.

And waited.

And played a bit of Scrabble to pass the time. The game ended sooner than I was expecting, when I put down some of the rude words that Granny had used when we'd played before: S*** B******* F****** and W*****. Only this time, because Mum and Dad were there, Granny was shocked by the swearing, shut up the board, said that she wasn't playing Scrabble with a ruffian and took herself off to bed.

And waited till morning.

It was late and early when they came back. A time of day that I didn't know existed – when the birds are singing but the sun hasn't come up yet. Only it wasn't just Mel and Will who walked across the field. There were three of them. Attached to Mel's arm was a creature with long matted hair, like one of those fur-balls that Napoleon chucks up on the carpet, thin legs, sloping shoulders and a thousand metal rings through his face. If you were cooking and didn't have a sieve, you could take all those rings out and strain the spaghetti through his face. Another funny thing to do would be to stand behind him with a magnet and pull his face into all sorts of unusual shapes; like a smile, for example. It could become an Olympic sport.

His name was Swamp Thing, because that's where Mel met him – crawling out of a swamp. And Thing, because there wasn't anything human about him – apart from his sandals. When he spoke he looked at the ground and made noises like he was clearing his throat. He made my big brother sound like a chatterbox. My guess is that Swamp Thing was abandoned as a baby and

brought up by sheep – hence the matted hair – and had an uncle who was a pig – hence the grunting. He also nervously drew shapes in the mud with his toe when you spoke to him, so I'm thinking that his first cousin was a chicken.

Mel and Will didn't want to go home! This is me – Big eyes; Big mouth; Big disbelief! That was all they had talked

about for the last don't-know-how-long. What had happened to change their minds? Mel had found a new boyfriend and would not be dragged away from the love of her life. I think Mel has got an illness. Some people are addicted to cigarettes, but Mel is addicted to boys. She gets through twenty a day! And William wanted to go back to the music festival – which was going on for weeks and weeks apparently, until all the bands and fans were buried alive in mud and then it would stop.

This is so TYPICAL of my big brother and sister, who ALWAYS do the OPPOSITE to what I want and change their minds without telling me. They are basically the two things I HATE most in the whole world. And in that I include funnel web spiders, and those grinning fish that swim up the end of your willy and build a love nest in your pee.

I think I've got that right.

how d'you think I feel?

Never thought I'd say that.

Luckily Mum and Dad were not in the mood for arguments. We were going home and that was that! HOORAH FOR PARENTS!

It didn't matter how much Mel and Will protested or how long their smackable faces became, they were not going to win.

'Then my beloved Swamp Thing can come home *with* us,' sulked Mel.

'But you've only just met him,' said Mum.

'Have you never heard of love at first sight?' cried Mel. We've all heard of love at first sight, but not with Swamp Thing. *Bath* at first sight, maybe! 'Anyway, he hasn't got a home of his own. His parents chucked him out.' →

BATH WATER AFTER SWAMP THING'S BATH

Mum was not to be moved. 'I'm sorry, Mel and Swamp Thing, but we don't have room in the car.'

'We'll ride in the caravan then.'

'We don't have room!' barked Dad. It was the first thing he'd said, but it had its effect.

With the rubbish, I should think.

Lo! A miracle!

Mel apologized to Swamp Thing for her ape-like parents, who were still stuck in the Stone Age, and gave him our address in Tooting.

'When will you be back?' he said. It was the first words I'd heard him speak.

'Tomorrow evening,' said Mum.

'Call you then,' he said, turning back towards the music. As he did so, something completely brilliant happened.

Three cars smashed through the gate into the field: two jeeps with soldiers in and a police car with its siren blaring. Swamp Thing took one look and ran. The rest of us watched in amazement, as the cars *didn't* give chase. Instead of bringing

down the one person who looked like a thief, they stopped next to Mum and Dad and ten men got out. Most of them were American soldiers. I could tell because they had no hair on their red necks and they wore their caps pulled down over their foreheads so that they had to peek out from under the peaks. Then they arrested Mum and Dad.

Dad was weeping and confessing all about bunking off Jury Service, and offering his hands up for handcuffs.

'Make it quick,' he blubbed. 'Just don't hurt me. I don't mind dying; it's the torture I can't take. Call me a coward . . .' So I called him a coward. That made him

cry even more. 'I'm sorry, kids. You should-n't have to see your father like this!'

Mel and Will agreed. They thought Dad was behaving like a baby and pretended not to be related to him by looking the other way. But they didn't fool anybody, because we were the only family camping in the field. And Mel clearly called him 'Dad' when she told him to wipe his nose.

Apparently, nobody knew anything about Dad's Jury Service. Mum and Dad were being arrested for attempted forced entry into a top secret American Army base.

'We have the whole ram raid incident on tape, sir,' said a shiny young American with spots. 'We need to establish why you escaped at such high veloc-ity when the VideoCop had given you an explicit order to remain where you were. Until we are fully cognisant of the facts and are fully satisfied that you are not enemies of the American People we will be taking you and your vehicles into custody. If you'd like to follow me, please.'

And off we went. The jeeps escorted our car and caravan through the lanes, while we three sat in the back of the car, not daring to say a word. Except Mel, of course.

'Did anyone else see that American driver give me the eye?' she said. 'I think he fancied me.'

If she was a cat, I'd have her neutered. Actually, what am I talking about? I'd just have done with it, put her in a sack and chuck her in the Thames. Kinder in the long run. For everyone.

The Thames

It was a lonely journey to the US base. We were all having private thoughts. Mine were about torture. I had visions of cold dark cells with stone floors and smelly mattresses infested with cockroaches. And peeing in a bucket. And dried bread with maggots in for breakfast, lunch and supper. And rats. And thumbscrews. And the Rack. And manacles with skeletons hanging off them. And the Chinese Water Torture. And unshaven guards who didn't brush their teeth. And no telly. The worst stuff you could imagine. I saw a film once called *Escape from Colditz*, in which British soldiers were taken prisoner and only gave their name, rank and cereal number. I don't know what a cereal number is but if they ask I shall say, 'Alistair Fury . . . Little Brother . . . Two Shredded Wheat.'

After that I shall just keep shtum.

We were split up when we got to the base. We were put in separate rooms and asked questions, which we did not have to answer, but I thought I probably should, seeing as the woman who was asking them had a gun. The rooms were quite nice and I got given a Coke. These were my questions (THEM) and answers (ME).

stealth bomber

THEM: 'What is your name?'

ME: 'Alistair Fury and NOT Alice, as my big brother and sister always call me, because they are ignorant and think they are being ho-so ho-so but they're not.'

THEM: 'Just answer the questions.'

ME: 'That's what I did.'

THEM: 'What are you doing here?'

ME: 'Being asked questions by you.'

THEM: 'No, not here. West Camel.'

ME: 'Who's Wes Camel?'

THEM: 'Just answer the questions.'

ME: 'I can't. I've never met a man called Camel.'

THEM: 'All right. Were you on vacation?'

ME: 'Is that a type of wart on your foot?'

THEM: 'No. A vacation is a holiday.'

ME: 'Yes and no.'

THEM: 'One answer please.'

ME: 'One? OK. *Nes*.'

THEM: 'Explain, please.'

ME: '*Please* is a polite word that you use when you want something that grown-ups don't want you to have.'

THEM: 'Wait here.'

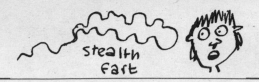

stealth
fart

At this point she left the room. She came back with a man in a white coat.

ME: 'Are you a doctor?'

DR: 'Yes.'

THEM: 'We'll ask the questions.'

ME: 'OK.'

DR: 'Have you ever taken a lie detector test?'

ME: 'Yes.'

DR & THEM [SURPRISED]: 'You *have*?'

ME: 'No. I was just testing the lie detector test. It failed.'

At this point I was strapped to the table and injected with something that made me sleep.

When I woke up I had told them everything I knew: that I loved Pamela Whitby (I said that several times apparently); that I hated Mum's cooking; that I wished Mel and Will were some-body else's big sister and brother; that newspapers lied, because Mum always sounded like 'the perfect mum' in every magazine article written about her, when she wasn't; that Dad was a coward; that Miss Bird was a witch with a desk full of compost; that Mrs Muttley had worms; that Granny had to go to the loo soon or she was going to explode; that I was going to be a world famous celebrity with a TVR and a tall girlfriend; that the Revengers were my blood brothers; and that an e-mail had been sent to the President of the United States from Mum's computer.

That was all they needed to know.

Mel and Will were arrested. Actually they were arrested already, so they were let go for half a second then arrested again.

'What for?' shouted Will.

The shiny-faced spot guard read the answer off a piece of paper.

'In this charge of grand treason it is hereby alleged that Melanie Fury (16) and William Fury (14) have committed an act of gross hostility towards the United States of America by sending an offensive e-mail to the White House in which they insulted the good name of the President of the United States and called his personal hygiene into question. The President would like it known that he is very particular about washing in those difficult-to-talk-about places at least twice a day. Melanie Fury and William Fury are clearly anarchists. As such, they have been classified as Highly Dangerous and must be liquidated pretty damn quick!'

It wasn't meant to be. I love making milkshakes.

I asked if liquidation meant putting Mel and Will through a blender, and if it did could I press the button. Nobody found this amusing.

They did, however, all look straight at me.

'What? WHAT?' I said. 'What have I done now? Why's it always MY fault?'

I was thrown into a cell on my own while everyone else was given a cup of milky coffee and a Rich Tea biscuit. In fact I think they probably got a burger too. With fries. CHEESY!

That's cheesy as in 'what a swizz', not a cheesy burger.

Still scared of torture. Especially when I heard a piercing scream down the corridor. My blood froze. Some poor innocent soul was being brutalized to within an inch of her life. I banged on the cell door, shouted for the guard and instantly became my father's son.

'I don't want to die!' I yelled in true cowardly Fury fashion. 'I'll tell you what you want to know, just don't pull out my fingernails like that poor old lady up the hall.

'That's your Granny,' said the guard. 'Constipation.'

STATEMENT FROM ALISTAIR FURY

I the undersigned do not want to go to prison for anything else that I have written, ever again. Is that clear? Undersigned

Alistair Fury

I was in that cell for days. I made one mark on the wall with the rubber heel of my shoe for every day I was in there. By the time the door was finally opened, and the bright lights blinded my pale and broken face, I had made forty-five marks!

'Sorry to have kept you,' said the guard lady. 'Here's your cheeseburger.'

Turns out I had only been in there for forty-five minutes. The cheeseburger was delicious, but they wouldn't give me another. I mentioned the Geneva Convention on the rights of prisoners of war, but they said that second helpings of cheeseburger weren't specifically covered.

I was then taken to see the camp commander, who was an *older* man with no hair on his red neck. He smoked a big cigar, which he called his *seagar*. He was much amused by this pronunciation and kept laughing at it. Suspect he has history of mental illness in family, but did not

MoM

PA

EL PRESIDENTE

He told me he would do this if I tried to run. Suspect this is example of excellent American sense of humour.

voice this, obviously, in case he stubbed his seagar out on my butt.

After relentless questioning I broke under the pressure and told him what the American nation wanted to know.

'I am a Revenger,' I said. I saw him take a step back. He was probably scared of my reputation. Saying the word Revenger is like saying Robin Hood or Hulk Hogan. It strikes fear into even the bravest of hearts. 'I do revenges against my big brother and sister, because I am their little brother and they treat me like scum. I sent the e-mail to get them into trouble, but you must never tell them or my mum and dad, or I'll be dead. OK?'

He promised to keep my secret.

We agreed to do the following: he would tell no one about our secret chat, if I would promise not to come back and take revenge on him. I promised. So he outlined what he could do for me. Turned out he was a little brother too.

'It won't do your big brother and sister any harm to spend the night in a cell,' he said. 'It's good for them at their age. Squatting on a bucket usually knocks the stuffing out of teenage rebels. And between you and me I think we'll bury the truth, just this once. I'll let them think it's their fault. Wha'd'ya say, pardner?'

So that's what happened. After all that time, my e-mail to the President had finally paid off! I had never felt more loved. Me and the United States of America standing shoulder to shoulder together as one!

DECLARATION OF INDEPENDENCE FOR NOT SO LITTLE BROTHERS ANY MORE

FROM THIS DAY FORTH AND SO ON AND SO ON, LITTLE BROTHERS IN BRITAIN AND AMERICA ARE NO LONGER A PERSECUTED MINORITY. WE STAND SHOULDER TO SHOULDER WITH EACH OTHER IN A LONG LINE OF SHOULDERS THAT CIRCLES THE WORLD LIKE A STRONG PIECE OF STRING.

Murderer or highwayman? I wonder.

The Fury family spent the night in prison, but not really. My cell was warm, comfortable and had colour TV. And best of all, it didn't smell of William!

12.01 p.m. – Spoke too soon. William has just been thrown in with me. A *real* prisoner needs his cell apparently.

Will just pushed me out of bed and made me sleep on the floor.

'Blimey! You really stink,' I said.

'If you're that bothered,' grumped my big brother, 'open the window!'

'Durrr! Like *hello*!' I replied. 'We're in prison here, William. Prison cells don't have windows.' Ours did though. So I opened it and fell asleep to the smell of cooked onions from the cookhouse instead of Will's smelly feet.

Later, when Will was snoring, I woke up again. It was cold on the floor. I asked Will if I could snuggle up for warmth. He said nothing so I climbed into the bed. He put his arm round me.

William woke up first and called me a big girl's blouse for having him in a sleepy hug.

I said, 'But I'm your little brother.'

Will slipped straight back into the old routine. 'So?' he sneered. 'I hate you.' No good has come from bucket squatting then.

Met up with rest of family. Granny thanked guards for such a comfortable night's sleep. 'And such clean toilets,' she said.

'Glad we could be of assistance,' said the camp commander.

'Oh no, nothing's changed,' complained Granny. 'Bowels are still dicky.'

Mum was a bit less nice. She wanted to know why we had been detained overnight when crashing into the fence had clearly been an accident.

'Just a precaution, ma'am,' said the commander, giving me a wink. 'You're free to go.'

'Begging your pardon, sir,' shouted a voice from the back of the room. It was the shiny young American with spots again. The one who'd arrested us in the field and read out the charge. 'Ma'am,' he said, 'it wasn't a precaution. Your youngest son wrote a rude e-mail to the President. He thinks our President stinks, which is a felony where I come from. This put your son, however temporarily, on a list of potential terrorists.'

'You promised nobody would tell!' I cried.

The commander shrugged his shoulders. 'I'm afraid that's Private Bush, son. He's a law unto himself. What we in the US Army call *keen*.'

'I'm sorry, Master Fury,' barked Private Bush, 'but I'd be failing in my duty as a perfect role model for today's youth if I didn't tell the truth!'

Private Bush's truth caused me nothing but grief. Now that I was exposed as the cause of the family's imprisonment I was blamed for everything that had ever gone

That's the back seat of the car, I mean ...
Although, they were pinching MY back seat as well!

wrong with the human race in general and the Fury family specifically.

American jeeps escorted us back to motorway, then left Mum and Dad to find their own way home. Mel and Will pinched <u>me on the back seat</u>, so much so that I screamed like a stuck pig. I was put in the

← STUCK

↙ GLUE

caravan with cowering pets and Granny, who was given strict instructions not to talk to me. We played Scrabble instead and Granny started off as she meant to continue by taking seventeen letters to start with.

'That's cheating!' I said.

She put her finger to her lips, then spelled out this with her letters: I THINK HE STINKS TOO. When I looked up from the board she was smiling.

Granny was back on the loo when we pulled into the drive at home. Dad misjudged the gateposts and wedged the caravan between them. I was desperate for House Points and tried to be helpful by getting out and pushing at the back, but Mum sent me to my room.

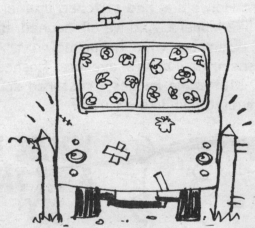

'What for?'
'For being thoroughly unpleasant, Alistair; for causing trouble *all* the time; for being cantankerous; for being irresponsible and stupid; and for lying.' I think she was upset because the caravan was stuck.

It was good to be back in the privacy of my room. I threaded landing phone under door and called Revengers. They were excited to hear my voice and to know that I was back, because now I could do the film and become rich and famous, and they could impress their friends by telling them that they knew me. I told them how the President prank had gone all the way to the White House and had stitched up Mel and Will like kippers. And we all laughed. But I don't remember what happened next. All I can see in my mind's eye are flashes of light, stuttering images, fractured sounds and matted hair like a furball.

WHAT I SAW IN MY MIND'S EYE

Shouting. Arm. Scratch. Dirt. Fist. Horsehair. Smack. Smell. Mud. Mud. Mel. Scream. Crash. Shriek. Thump in back. Phone fall. Tinkle-bell. Tiny voice running in a tunnel. Arm across chest. Ralph calling. Door slam. Dad wails. Jangle of jewellery.

Hot breath. Footsteps. Will trips. Mum shouts. Will cries. Harder shove. Feet slip. Stairs rise. Swear words. Wooden box. Lid. Wall. Chipped paint. Old games – lacrosse, rugby, tennis, Frisbee . . .

And then, there I was; at the top of the stairs with Swamp Thing standing behind me. He was holding me against him with one arm across my chest and my family standing at the foot of the stairs looking up. Looking worried and scared. And William's mouth was bleeding.

Thinking we would take for ever getting home from West Camel, Swamp Thing, and Swamp Thing's best mate Fungus, had rushed up to London to burgle us. Only we'd come back sooner than they'd thought and caught them at it. In their panic to get out, I was taken hostage.

'Don't come near us!' shouted Swamp Thing from the top of the stairs, 'or the kid gets it.'

'Gets it with what?' said Mum calmly. I think she thought it was a joke. Which in a way it was. Swamp Thing was holding a Frisbee to my neck.

'I was looking for a baseball bat,' he said, 'but I couldn't find one.'

'Try the tennis racket,' I said. 'That would hurt me a lot more than a Frisbee.'

'Do you think so?' said Swamp Thing.

'Oh yes,' I said.

So Fungus swapped the Frisbee for a

tennis racket, which Swamp Thing held menacingly at my throat.

The tennis racket of DEATH

'Thanks,' he said to me. 'I'm not very good at kidnap. It's my first time.'

'You're not very good at burglary either,' said my mum, 'or you wouldn't have got caught.'

'My first time burgling too.' Suddenly, he turned nasty. 'But don't think that means I'm going to make mistakes, because I'm not. I've thought this through.'

'I'm sure you have,' said Mum sarcastically.

Sometimes parents are so stupid. I mean, there is a time for sarcasm and there is a time for sweetness and light. When your youngest son is being held hostage with a deadly tennis racket inches from his throat that is not the time to be sarcastic. I could have got seriously

First sensible thing I'd heard him say.

volleyed. Anyway, the result of the sarcasm was that Swamp Thing got cross and confused.

'Shut up!' he shouted. 'Shut up all of you.'

That included Mel, who was sobbing. 'Don't you love me any more, Swamp Thing?'

← 'I only just met you,' he replied.

'Now here's the deal. Me and Fungus are leaving right now and we're taking the car.'

'You can't,' said Mum. 'The car's blocked in by the caravan, which is jammed in the gates.'

'Sorry,' said Dad, who was cowering coward-like in a corner trying not to annoy the villains.

'We're not amateurs,' said Swamp Thing.

'Get us a helicopter or a speedboat!'

Even I laughed at that. 'We're not on a river, here,' I said. 'And we're really going to know how to get a helicopter, aren't we? My dad runs a leisure centre. Mum cooks on TV. She could bake you a cake in the shape of a helicopter.'

Swamp Thing kicked the carpet like I sometimes do when life doesn't go the way you want it to. 'OK. Give us all your money. We'll make our own way out of here.'

'How much?' said Mum.

Swamp Thing looked at Fungus, who shrugged his shoulders. 'A million pounds!'

Both parents laughed, which was a disappointing reaction. This was no laughing matter. My life was hanging by a thread and they were holding that thread in their hands. Only they could save me and pull me out of the fires of Hell, but with every laugh they uttered, that precious thread of life slipped further and further through their fingers.

'It's not that funny,' I shouted. 'At least make it look like you want to save me!'

According to Mum, the cash-flow problem was all tied up with *Towed in the Hole!* If Mum had heard from Michael, if the BBC had commissioned her series, things might have been different.

'I might be able to give you a few hundred pounds,' she said. 'But if you're serious that it's a million or nothing, I'll just go and pack Alistair's suitcase, because he'll be living with *you* from now on, permanently.'

So the truth was out! This was what Mum had wanted all along. Swamp Thing and Fungus were part of a plot to get me out of the family and dump me in an orphanage with a forged passport, which would say that I, like Jesus, was born without parents!

But Swamp Thing didn't look like a conspirator. He was anxiously biting his lip-ring. 'I don't believe you,' he said to Mum. 'You're a celebrity. You must earn fortunes.'

'I earn a comfortable living,' said Mum, like she was chatting away at a coffee morning, 'but my ingredients aren't cheap. A starter with truffles, for example, sets me back forty quid.'

Dad put his hand up. 'And a leisure centre manager earns peanuts!' he said.

'That's because a monkey could do it,' said Fungus, which we all thought was very funny and everyone laughed. Everyone except Dad, of course. He just looked hurt.

'OK. So how much *will* you pay?' asked Swamp Thing. 'Hundreds, thousands? Give us a clue.'

'Not thousands,' said Mum.

I had to jump in here. 'Now hang on a minute,' I cried. 'You can't negotiate for my life. When we were in the caravan and I asked you what you'd give to get Napoleon and Mr E back, you said everything: your house, your car, all your money. You didn't put a limit on it!'

It is a sad day when you become just another number in your parents' eyes. I could also see my big brother and sister mentally picking through all the precious stuff in my room so that when I was dead they could take what they wanted. I bet they'll fight over the sofa. I hope it splits right down the middle while they're tugging it from both ends and fills up the house with feathers, which float down their throats and suffocate them. There have been many times in my life when I have felt unloved, but this one takes the biscuit!

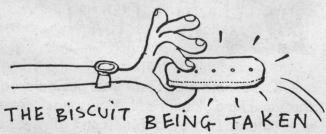

THE BISCUIT BEING TAKEN

And look how they turned out.

Negotiations were getting nowhere. Neither side wanted me. So I called a time-out and asked Swamp Thing and Fungus for a private word.

'You do realize you're wasting your breath,' I said. 'Mum and Dad will *never* pay. I'm hated by everyone. They *want* me to go!'

'Oh no,' said Swamp Thing. 'I forgot. You're a Little Brother, aren't you?' Swamp Thing and Fungus looked depressed. They were both little brothers too.

'We can forget the money then,' said Swamp Thing.

'Ask for something they *might* swap me with,' I suggested.

'Something useful, you mean?' said Fungus. 'Like a bag of sugar?'

'I'm not *that* unpopular!' I protested. 'Like the caravan. You could live in it.'

After a couple of minutes Swamp Thing and Fungus agreed. The caravan would be cool.

Mum and Dad said 'Fine!' and threw in

the car as well – 'if you can push it out from between the gateposts!' Sounds generous, but the car was a heap of tat really. Worth zilch after Dad had smashed it up on the roundabout. Mum said she didn't care what happened to the caravan now that *Towed in the Hole!* had fallen through.

So the deal was that they would put back everything they'd stolen, then we would unhitch the caravan from the car, push it into the road, hitch up the caravan again and let them drive off completely free.

We went outside. Mum, Dad, Will and Mel first. Me, Swamp Thing, the tennis racket and Fungus second. There was a surprise on the pavement. The press was there to cover TOOTING TV COOK IN UNLOVED LITTLE BROTHER HOSTAGE NIGHTMARE. I could tell as I walked out that the press wanted me dead, because that would make a better story. They were shouting things like: 'Any last words, Alistair?' 'Will you use that racket if you have to, Mr Swamp Thing?' and 'Show us your forehand!'

There was a TV crew there as well, interviewing Ralph and Aaron. ———→

This was the biggest surprise

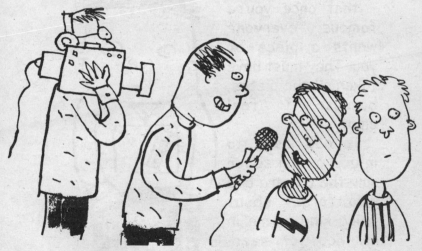

They gave me the big thumbs-up and grinned when they saw me.

'When you were kidnapped you left the phone off the hook,' shouted Aaron. 'We heard everything. So we called the local papers.'

'And I called the TV people,' said Ralph.

'You didn't think of calling the police?' I shouted back.

'No,' said Ralph. 'This was our chance to become celebrities like you. And it's working, look!' Everyone wanted to talk to them about their friendship with me.

It's true what Richard and Judy say about celebrityhood – that once you're famous, everyone wants a piece of you. They must have taken all the pieces, because I feel empty.

To add insult to injury my big sister saw the camera and also forgot about being kind to me in my hour of need. She rushed over to the interviewer, pushed Ralph and Aaron to one side, and told the interviewer that he could interview *her* now, because she was the big sister and anything she said would be miles more interesting and true. I knew what was going on. She hadn't got into the Toopac Nijinski film because of her stinky acting, so this was her second try at proving that she could be a famous actress. How did I know that? She asked for a tissue from make-up to dry her eyes. Then, when the camera was rolling, jabbed her finger in her eye to make herself cry. Not only that, but after the interview she asked the interviewer if her tragic, grief-filled tears had been convincing.

'Not really,' he said.

'It's all right,' she said, 'I won't get big-headed. You can tell me I was brilliant if you like.'

'But you weren't,' said the interviewer.

So she rammed his microphone down his trousers and told him that he was the worst interviewer she had ever been interviewed by and from now on should stick to interviewing his own bottom.

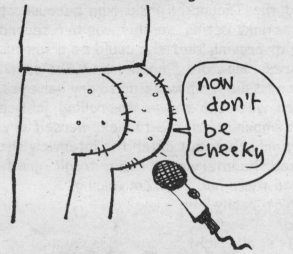

now don't be cheeky

We pushed the caravan into the road and did all the re-hitching. Fungus jumped into the driving seat and I thought my ordeal was over. Not a bit of it. Swamp Thing suddenly pushed down on the top of my head and squeezed me into the back of the car. Mum and Dad jumped forward, but Swamp Thing backed them off with the racket.

'What are you doing?' I shouted. 'The deal was the caravan and car, not me.'

'Change of plan,' said Swamp Thing.

'You're staying with us until we're safely away from here.'

Suddenly I was scared. 'Are you going to kill me?' I asked. Swamp Thing said nothing, which I took for a *yes*. 'But you can't! See those two boys out there,' I cried. 'They're the Revengers. They'll come after you and revenge themselves on you for the rest of your lives.' Fungus laughed. 'All right,' I said, trying a new idea. 'I'm going to be a film star next week. How about I give you half my fee for not killing me?'

'Now we're talking,' smiled Swamp Thing. 'How much is the fee?'

'Well, I don't actually know,' I said, 'but Tom Cruise gets twenty-five million dollars per movie. Now, admittedly I'm not as famous as him, and I've never acted before, but it's still a film, so it's got to be a hundred thousand pounds, hasn't it?'

Yet

Swamp Thing was chuffed with fifty thousand, and promised not to kill me. My relief was short-lived, however, when I suddenly remembered that Mum wouldn't let me do the film. 'No film, no money,' I explained. 'You're going to have to issue a new set of demands.'

Swamp Thing shouted his new demands from the back of the car.

'You want WHAT now?' shouted Mum.

'We want the car and the caravan and we want you to let Alistair make his film next week.'

'Or what?' she said.

Swamp Thing looked uncomfortable. 'Or we'll . . .'

'Go on, say it,' I whispered. But he couldn't. The word stuck in his throat. 'Or he'll kill me,' I shouted.

'Ah,' said Mum, 'that changes things rather.' She paused. 'If they're going to kill you, Alistair, I suppose you *can* make your film after all!'

Now that is what we celebrities call a hole in one!

So I got out of the car and Swamp Thing and Fungus drove off with our caravan. Dad burst into tears from all the worry and stress, while Mum gave me a soppy kiss and marched back into the house to answer the phone. Mel hated me again for doing the film and Will awkwardly shook my hand, which was nice.

It was a confusing phone call for Mum:

1. The good news was that Michael had been in to see the BBC and they *did* want *Towed in the Hole!* after all. Cue smiles and over-the-top rejoicing!

2. The bad news was that he had been trying to call Mum for the last three days but her mobile had always been engaged. Mum blew her top and looked daggers at Mel, who simply pointed her finger at me. 'I've just been released from a life-and-death hostage situation!' I cried. 'Have you no heart, sister mine?' Clearly not.

3. The even worse news was that now that Mum had been given the all clear to make *Towed in the Hole!* she no longer had a caravan to be towed in.

It was understandable that Mum should lose her rag and that she and I should have another chase-upstairs-with-spiky-hairbrush moment. She had been under a small amount of pressure recently. So getting the programme then losing it within seconds was bound to play tricks with her mind. Luckily just before she whacked me, I remembered something important.

'Granny!' I yelled. 'Where's Granny?'

'In the caravan,' gasped Mum, looking horribly guilty. 'I left her on the loo.'

'That's all right then,' I said. 'She'll be back in three hours.'

She was back in two. Swamp Thing and Fungus listened to her bowels for an hour, then played three games of Scrabble and gave in. They returned the car and the caravan and hoped out loud that they would never meet the Fury family again.

'Nice polite boys,' said Granny, as she stood on the doorstep and waved them off. 'A bit dirty, but so is William and that doesn't make him bad, does it? Oooh!' She grabbed her stomach. 'Holiday over. I can feel a stirring!' And she rushed inside to bags the loo.

Harmony has returned to the House of Fury.

SATURDAY (DAY 8)

Woke late after trauma of kidnap. Missed breakfast. Missed lunch too, for which I give thanks to God. Mum outstripped herself today with a new dish for her new cooking programme. The ingredients were a subtle combination of local produce from rural Buckinghamshire and Salisbury Zoo. It was called Liver and Blackbird Beak in a Glazed Opossum Sauce. Think she has gone slightly off her sweet trolley.

OK- you think you can draw that better the be my guest !

2 p.m. - Dad took phone call from some very low-down person working for director. It is my call for filming tomorrow. That means I am working on a *Sunday*, which is the most exotic day of the week to work, when most normal people don't. But that is the film business for you, darling. Quite mad!

I have to be on set by nine o'clock, in a disused warehouse in Wandsworth. Oh yes, yes, yes! Celebrityhood! The glitz, the glam, the tinsel and teeth! I feel superior already! Must get bus at eight o'clock if not to be late.

As all great actors do, I spent day preparing for my role. Ate lots of crisps and sweets and drank lots of cola to strengthen voice.

BBURRP!

Also watched lots of telly to see if I could pick up any tips from other actors. To be honest, and without being modest, I don't think there's much I can learn from other actors. I have the gift of acting in me and that's not something you can copy off jobbing soap stars.

8 p.m. – Early to bed. Must have bright, sparkling eyes for camera. Surprised at how calm I am. No nerves at all. Must be a natural!

9 p.m. – Can't sleep.

10 p.m. – Can't sleep.

11 p.m. – Still can't sleep.

2 a.m. – Have just had awful nightmare.

MY AWFUL NIGHTMARE WHAT I'VE JUST HAD

I was on set filming my film and discussing my very important role with my world-famous director, when Pamela Whitby came out of her dressing room. Could not believe my eyes.

'What are you staring at, Alistair?' she purred. 'Is it my silky hair, my lovely long legs or my peek-a-boo negligée promising so much more than just Scrabble?'

'None of them,' I said. 'Your dressing room's bigger than mine!'

4 a.m. – Heard milkman arrive.

SUNDAY (DAY 9)

Am going to be so busy today that I will have very little time for tedious tittle-tattle of diary. Sorry, fans, but greatness and immorality call!

8 a.m. – On bus.

9 a.m. – On set.

10 a.m. – On phone to agent – or would be if I had one. This is no film. This cheesy bit of silliness is an advert for a deodorant! Sense of doom about this. Feel humiliation pending. Suddenly wish I'd stayed on holiday in caravan.

1 p.m. – Have just worked nearly ONE hour without a break or anyone smiling at me. Must get 'People to smile at me and tell me I'm good!' clause included in next contract. Plus lunch was dried cheese sandwich. Not even a sniff of champagne and oysters.

5 p.m. – Finished advert. Hope film is ruined. Hope the dark room where they make the pictures is so dark that the man

Immortality, I mean.

HUMILIATION

who sticks the pictures on the film cannot see what he is doing and sticks the pictures on a big rat who runs into the sewers and is never seen again!

5.15 p.m. – Got bus home. Was I imagining it or were people staring at me?

5.17 p.m. – They *were* staring. Little me *was* a celebrity after all!

5.18 p.m. – Realized I was still wearing make-up.

5.19 p.m. – Stood up and told bus that I was an actor, not a girl, which explained why I was wearing eyeshadow. People stopped staring and got off bus.

6 p.m. – Revengers called to find out how first day on Ladder of Fame shaped up. Told them I didn't want to speak about it.

6.02 p.m. – Revengers arrived at house to speak about it.

6.05 p.m. – Full story out. This is it:

Toopac Nijinski was famous for being two things: a boy and a girl. He was brought up as a boy until he was ten, when someone realized that he was in fact a girl. So he switched to being a girl called Miss Toopac, took ballet lessons, wore a tutu and danced for the Royal Ballet. I was chosen to play Toopac because director thought I had something of a boy and something of a girl about me. The advert shows Toopac wearing deodorant as a boy in a football kit, followed by Toopac wearing deodorant as a girl in a tutu. The final line is: *'No matter whether you're a boy or a girl, Desert Dry deodorant is the one for you.'*

241

'It's a deodorant that either sex can use,' I explained.

Ralph and Aaron said they'd understood.

'But you don't even wear deodorant,' said Aaron. 'You're too little.'

'I know!' I cried. 'That's what makes it all so stupid. You don't think I'm going to look like a girl in a pink tutu, do you?'

Ralph and Aaron raised their eyebrows and looked at the floor.

'Is it just a telly campaign or posters as well?' asked Ralph.

'Posters as well,' I said glumly. 'There's going to be no escaping it.'

'Still,' said Aaron, 'look on the bright side. At least you got paid well.'

'Thirty-three pounds and a free deodorant,' I told them.

Then Ralph looked at Aaron and Aaron looked at Ralph and they both got up and left.

Am now dreading the rest of the holiday.

'Alas, poor Alistair. I knew him well.'

Advert has appeared. Spent day in bedroom.

Never never never again! This is not the sort of fame I was dreaming about. People stop me in the street to LAUGH at me! I think deodorants stink!

Am cancelling the rest of the summer holidays and never going out again. As a protest against a world that is mocking me, I am going to sit at home and do nothing.

Did something today. Took bellybutton
fluff out of bellybutton.

Put it back.

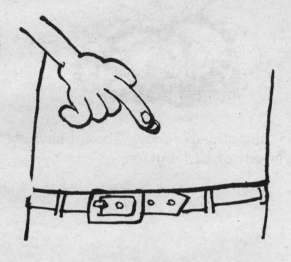

Took it out again. Wrapped it up and gave it to Mel with a note:

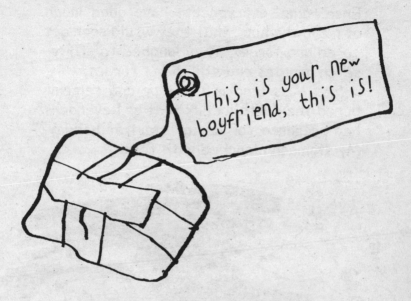

First day back at school. Felt like idiot in the playground. Encouraged tutu jokes. Encouraged everyone to have good laugh at me in the hope that they would soon get bored and forget. They laughed for fifty-seven minutes and still didn't forget.

Met Miss Bird in corridor and remembered the dustbin desk that us Revengers had prepared for her at start of holiday. My stomach clenched with fear.

'Good morning, Miss Toopac,' she sneered. Then *she* laughed, and with that laugh all fear disappeared. My belly was re-fired with revenge. She deserved everything she was going to get!

And get it she did. Her desk was like an elephant had lifted its tail and parked its lunch under the lid. There was a thick brown puddle of rotting juices underneath and a mushroom field growing on top. It had a smell that reminded me of Will's trainers with Will's pants and socks stuffed inside! Miss Bird had a blue fit. She couldn't speak for ten minutes. When she did it was to tell the child or children who did it to stand up.

Ralph, Aaron and me stayed put. There's no way the old witch is ever going to find out who did it.

Oops! Got to hand my holiday project in now. This be my final entry . . . tree . . . tree . . . tree . . . tre . . . tr . . . t.

BYEEEEEEEEEEE!!!!!!!!!

-25/10
Fail, fail, fail, fail, fail, fail, fail!

Not only is this holiday diary a pack of lies, but you are in deep trouble, Dumbo. Or should I call you Mr Stupid? I now know who composted my desk! You will live to regret writing everything down. Trust me. Let's start with a few Saturday morning detentions. Then we can talk about redecorating my flat, doing my weekly shopping, weeding my garden, washing my smalls and rubbing my feet with alcohol.
   Miss Bird

   PS If you still have that deodorant I suggest you wear it all the time. From now on, Fury, I'm going to make you sweat!

ABOUT THE AUTHOR

Jamie Rix originally started writing and producing comedy for TV and radio, including such programmes as *Alas Smith and Jones,* starring Mel Smith and Griff Rhys Jones, and *Radio Active.* Jamie's first children's book, *Grizzly Tales for Gruesome Kids,* was published in 1990 and won the Smarties Prize Children's Choice Award. Since then he has written children's books for a wide variety of age groups, including *Johnny Casanova - the Unstoppable Sex Machine,* for older readers, and several sequels to the *Grizzly Tales...* This book and its sequels have been adapted into an award-winning television animation series.

Jamie's first book for Young Corgi was the very funny *One Hot Penguin,* which *The Times Educational Supplement* called 'an excellent book with a double-edged resolution'. His latest project is a series of books containing THE WAR DIARIES OF ALISTAIR FURY - the hilarious account of an eleven-year-old boy desparate for revenge on his older brother and sister.

Jamie is married with two grown-up sons and, like Alistair Fury, he lives in Tooting, London.

THE WAR DIARIES OF ALISTAIR FURY

Bugs on the Brain

Jamie Rix

BONSAI! THIS IS WAR

My big brother and sister, William and Mel, may be older than me and biggerer than me, but they're not cleverer than me. Just because the chips of the world are stacked against me like a potato mountain doesn't mean they can beat me. Revenge will be mine!

Or rather mine and the Revengers', and a boa constrictor called Alfred's. Let loose the snakes of doom and see how they like it then! I shall have my revenge before you can say 'peanut butter and jam sandwiches'! Actually I shouldn't have mentioned peanut butter and jam sandwiches. Forget you ever read that. If you don't, I may have to kill you.

The first book in a brilliant and hilarious series by award-winning comic writer, Jamie Rix.

CORGI YEARLING BOOKS
ISBN 0440 864763

THE WAR DIARIES OF ALISTAIR FURY

Dead Dad Dog

Jamie Rix

LIFE IS PANTS

Mum, Dad, William and Mel are ill. It's 'Fetch this, Alistair; bring that, Alistair...' all day long. Huh! Do they think I'm their slave? I'm far too busy sorting out my own problems. First, there's Mrs Muttley and her persistent piano lessons. (I don't know why she won't believe that my fingers have fallen off.) Then there's the bright yellow trousers that my mum had bought me - and the photo of me taken without any trousers on at all! To say nothing of Great-Uncle Crawford and the disappearing suit, or Miss Bird and the repulsive recipes...

The only kind ones in this family are the pets - and a vampire dog and an unstable cat aren't much use. Luckily I've still got my real friends - the Revengers - and a ghost of an idea of how to get my own back on the family.

The second book in a brilliant and hilarious series by award-winning comic writer, Jamie Rix.

CORGI YEARLING BOOKS
ISBN 0440 864771

THE WAR DIARIES OF ALISTAIR FURY

Kiss of Death
Jamie Rix

British beef and French mustard
Go together like snails and custard

I know that sounds like one of Mum's gross TV-chef recipes but actually it's a love poem for Giselle, our French exchange girl. *Everyone's* trying to impress her - my brother William, the Revengers, Colin the builder - they're all after her.

I thought if I said something beautiful to Giselle in French she'd like me best, but I could only think of "Bonjovi, j'apple Alistair". That didn't exactly set her heart on fire... unlike the shed which turned into the barbecue at Mum's boring Bondi Beach party! Me and the Revengers want to throw a proper party with people our own age, kissing and crisps. If Giselle comes to that, she'll be able to see how attractive and mature I am. Ooh la la!

The third book in a brilliant and hilarious series by award-winning comic writer, Jamie Rix.

CORGI YEARLING BOOKS
ISBN 0440 86478X

THE WAR DIARIES OF ALISTAIR FURY

Tough Turkey

Jamie Rix

Christmas is the best time of year. Only dead people or people without a telly don't enjoy Christmas. Or little brothers (i.e. me!). My family are doing their best to ruin my childhood. I wish I was King Herod and could do them in.

My big brother and sister are making sure I get no presents. Mum has got a celebrity magazine taking festive photos of the family at war. The turkey's been dumped for a goose. Dad's turning green, and orange, and ever so slightly lobster as well. And Gran is going abroad – we hope.

But with a ton of help from my fellow Revengers, Mr E and the little baby Wayne...

Hark the herald angels sing
I will get my revenge in!

Another hilarious instalment in this brilliant series by award-winning comic writer, Jamie Rix.

CORGI YEARLING BOOKS
ISBN 0440 864798